A WOMAN'S PLACE

Sarah Courtney has lived with her aunt and uncle, a prosperous merchant, since her father died a year ago. When the handsome and wealthy Ross Balfour catches her eye, she has no expectation of marrying him — until they accidentally fall into a compromising situation, and he offers for her hand to save her reputation. Ross's plan is for the union to be a sham so that Sarah can receive her inheritance and fulfil her dream of opening an apothecary's shop. Love will never enter into it . . . or will it?

WENDY KREMER

A WOMAN'S PLACE

Complete and Unabridged

LINFORD
Leicester

First published in Great Britain in 2019

First Linford Edition
published 2020

A catalogue record for this book is available
from the British Library.

ISBN 978–1–4448–4579–2

Published by
Ulverscroft Limited
Anstey, Leicestershire
Set by Words & Graphics Ltd.
Anstey, Leicestershire
Printed and bound in Great Britain by
T. J. International Ltd., Padstow, Cornwall

This book is printed on acid-free paper

Handsome Stranger

When they were introduced, Ross Balfour's dark eyes were the first thing that impressed her. Sarah couldn't define their exact colour but she did notice that his hair shone like raven's feathers as he stood with his back to the hall's glowing wall-lamps.

He viewed her with friendliness and interest. Most people ignored her after being introduced, especially when they realised she was a minor member of Uncle Aidan's family.

Ross Balfour was above average height — Sarah barely reached his shoulders — and he was clean shaven. That was unusual in this day and age.

Her impression was a handsome man with a slight tan, who had an impeccable sense of fashion. His

1

evening dress of black and white was flawless. His bearing was confident and he was clearly at ease with himself and his surroundings.

She'd been crossing the hall when her uncle was accompanying him on his way to the meet the other guests. They had to pass Sarah, so out of politeness, her uncle introduced him briefly, then urged him along.

A moment later her aunt came looking for her.

'Sarah, tell Mrs McGregor to serve dinner in twenty minutes. All the guests are here. And tidy your hair.' She looked at her niece and sighed. 'It is such a beautiful colour, but it looks flimsy as soon as it works loose. At present it's nothing short of tousled.'

'Yes, Aunt Sybil.' Sarah couldn't help the fact that her hair was sometimes unmanageable. It was usually gathered tightly in a chignon at the base of her neck, and then curls, ringlets or plaits were arranged on the sides, according to the time of day, and the occasion. At

2

the moment, tiny curls were trying to escape their confining clips. She hurried to warn Bessie that the company was already gathering in the dining-room and she could begin to serve the evening meal.

Bessie was busy giving the assistant cook last minute instructions and inspecting the waiting dishes. She gave Sarah a broad smile and pinched her cheek.

'Thank you, lassie. You'd better join the others or someone else will nab your place.'

Sarah pulled a face.

'To be honest, Bessie, I wouldn't care. These dinner parties are so boring and so stiff.'

'Aye, well! Your uncle is one of the biggest jute manufacturers in the town. He needs to entertain both his customers and competitors alike, to know where he stands. Men in his position always do. More business is done over the dining table than you can imagine. I don't suppose your aunt minds if, as always, you disappear when the men join the women in the drawing-room for coffee.'

Absent-mindedly, she tucked some loose strands of hair behind Sarah's ears and smoothed the sides of her draped green skirt before she turned back to the growing activity and noise in the kitchen behind her.

Sarah joined the family members and their guests. She noted that some of them were sneaking glances at the place cards and politely helped them find their chosen seat. She knew where everyone would sit, because she had helped her aunt to set the table.

The most important guests had interesting neighbours. Anyone else, like herself, filled the gaps. Sarah had a local preacher on one side, and an overweight banking acquaintance of her uncle on the other.

Sarah was sitting opposite her cousin Abigail, and Abigail had Mr Ross Balfour on her right — the man she'd met in the hallway. He was an unfamiliar face, and now she recalled once more what her aunt had mentioned about him when they were arranging the table.

According to Aunt Sybil he was very rich, even though he was still in his early thirties. He was a foreign trader who spent his life in the Far East and his interesting background and colourful history made him a popular dinner guest.

When he was present, there was never a lack of out-of-the-ordinary discussions about the colonies, foreign business and other pertaining concerns.

Sarah regarded him carefully. He seemed to be a thoughtful conversationalist. Abigail appeared quite content.

He looked across the table, noticed her watching him, and his eyes twinkled. Sarah looked down quickly. She knew it was ill-mannered to stare, but she was bored, and her neighbours were such uninspiring communicators.

She had almost given up trying to show interest in such things as the

5

monthly meeting of the local church committee, or the flagging sale of stock for the new railway being built between Stockport and Manchester.

She wondered what Ross Balfour thought of Abigail. Abigail had pleasing features but she was pretty, not beautiful. He had probably met dozens of more attractive women. Abigail was easily distracted, and she also hadn't read more than a handful of books in her whole life. A stranger would struggle to find mutual themes that would interest her but he seemed to be trying.

Abigail's lack of interest in books was something Sarah found hard to understand. Sarah guessed, as she viewed them, that her aunt was hoping for a good match for Abigail. She was hoping for someone like Ross Balfour, whose riches matched, or even surpassed, that of her husband.

Sarah ate, listened, tried to make appropriate commentaries to the men to her left and right but, as she was a

skirt drawn back and bunched at the rear, rustled as she moved towards the large desk. A sound disturbed her and she whirled to find Ross Balfour sitting in one of the high-backed armchairs alongside the fireplace. The colour flooded her cheeks.

'Oh! I wasn't expecting to find anyone here any more.'

The flickering flames of the fire threw shades of colours across his face and into the recesses of the chair. He was smoking a cigarillo and blew some blue smoke into the air.

'So I gather! We have been introduced and I recall that you are a relation, but can't remember your name.'

She steadied.

'Sarah Courtney. I'm Abigail's cousin.'

'Are you on a visit?'

She was surprised that he was curious enough to ask.

'No, not on a visit, I live here. I've lived with my uncle's family since my father died, over a year ago.'

Ross scrutinised, her eye-catching appearance. A lamp on the desk gave him a better view of Sarah than she had of him. Her face was delicate with a generous curved mouth. Her eyes were cool grey and their shifting colour reminded him of the loch near his childhood home. She had a slender, willowy, figure.

'And . . . do you like it here in Dundee?' he asked quietly.

She realised that polite society would demand a positive answer. She was too direct, and honest, not to grab the chance to reply truthfully. He seemed different from anyone she had ever met before.

'My aunt and uncle are very kind to me, but I don't particularly like Dundee and that is all I've seen of Scotland since I arrived. I preferred it where we lived before, in Leicester. Dundee at this time of year is dark when we get up, cold and miserable all day long, and dark again early in the evening.'

He smothered a laugh, and his white

teeth flashed in the firelight.

'Ah, well, it probably does seem quite austere and bleak to an English woman, but autumn and winter are never pleasant anywhere in Britain, are they?'

'I love autumn's colours and the snow in winter,' she replied with an inkling of defiance. 'I only mean that further south the temperatures and the winds are milder. Here the wind stiffens your bones before you've gone ten yards. But I only know Dundee, and everyone extols the beauty of the Lowlands, and the Highlands. People also say the Scottish islands are very wild and beautiful. Perhaps I'll see them one day and appreciate Scotland better.'

He felt a need to defend his homeland.

'There is breathtaking scenery nearby and the sun does shine here, too. When the skies are blue, it is a special kind of blue, one I only find here. You might not believe it, but I actually miss miserable weather sometimes.'

11

She shrugged.

'Do you? How strange, but if you live in foreign climes I expect it will be part of your hankering reminiscences! I must say, it was nicer in spring and it was almost mild some days in summer, although I've discovered it is never wise to dress frivolously.'

His eyes were bright with merriment as he considered the way her shining tresses framed her face. He wished he could reach out and feel its texture.

Sarah wondered if he thought she was completely irrational.

'People tell me Scotland does have sunny, warmer weather,' she added quickly. 'I just haven't been around long enough yet.' His mouth twitched with amusement but he remained silent. She ploughed on. 'I've heard that you live, and work, in the Far East, Mr Balfour. That must be exciting.'

He nodded and noted that she had remembered his name. He enjoyed her spontaneity and lively conversation. Unlike most of the women he'd met since he returned, she could probably hold an intelligent conversation. He was sure Sarah Courtney was not fishing for attention, either. He had enough experience to judge that.

'In Singapore and Hong Kong.'

'Oh, how thrilling. Hong Kong is a relatively young colony still, isn't it? It must be interesting to be part of its growth and development. I've read about Singapore, too. It must be grand to live in such places. You don't need to worry about fog, rain, snow, or icy winds in either of those spots.'

He chuckled.

'No, but you worry about hurricanes, fierce typhoons, uncomfortable temperatures, cholera, outbreaks of the plague, dysentery, malaria, and lots of other unpleasant things instead.'

She challenged his words.

'Ah, but you are generously compensated by beautiful flowers, plants, colourful and exotic surroundings, a distinctive atmosphere, and a contrasting culture — although I only presume so because of what I've read in books or in newspapers,' she hastened to add.

He stared at her silently for a moment. She was an interesting woman.

'Most people get used to the heat eventually, but it does have drawbacks. It is not just romantic adventure, Miss Courtney. Living and working in such localities can be risky and exhausting. There is appalling poverty and injustice, tropical diseases, and a lot of puffed-up beings who think they are pint-size gods.'

His eyes quickened with mischief.

'You seem extremely interested and well-informed. Most people don't have the slightest clue, or care about Singapore or Hong Kong. They often don't know where it is on the map, unless they are soldiers, politicians, businessmen, or bankers.'

She gestured in a wide arc with her hand.

'This room is full of information, and I always read my uncle's newspaper when he has finished with it. Bessie gives it to me before she uses it to light the stove in the kitchen. I love reading, especially about foreign places like Hong Kong, even if I'll never see them.

'I think my uncle and I are the only ones who ever read books or papers in this house. For me, books are windows on another world outside of these walls, and outside of this town.'

'I gather that your mother is dead? If she was still alive there'd be no need for you to live with your uncle.'

'Yes. She died ten years ago. She had inflammation of the lungs and even my father couldn't help her. He was an apothecary,' she explained, 'a very good one. People trusted him and loved him for his knowledge and help.'

'And when he died, you came to live with the Courtneys?'

'Yes. If I were a man, I could have kept the shop, but a woman has no choice,' she stated, trying not to sound ungrateful. 'I worked with my father. I watched him, and learned from him. I already knew a great deal about medicine and mixtures by the time he died. I loved him very much and the work he did was important. He cared about people and he helped anyone, even if they couldn't always pay for his help.' She looked down for a second, lost in memories.

For some reason he wanted to lighten her gloominess.

'The Chinese use medicines and treatments that go back thousands of years,' he declared. 'They employ a lot of plants and natural substances in their mixtures. It is surprising how effective they are.'

'Yes, I've read about that, too. If people were not doubters about so many things, we could combine all helpful knowledge for everyone's benefit.'

'I presume your father was not interested in the jute industry? If you are a Courtney, he was one, too.'

'He was Uncle Aidan's brother. Papa told me that when he visited Bangladesh as a young man, he found it difficult

16

afterwards to accept that workers there were paid a pittance for producing and shipping the raw jute. He argued about the working conditions in the factory here, too, declaring they were unnecessarily bad and unhealthy.

'My grandfather agreed to finance his studies with a famous doctor in Edinburgh, because he saw he would only cause disruption and discord in the company. Eventually my father decided he could help ordinary people most by becoming an apothecary. Sometimes I think he knew more about medicine than our local doctor.'

Ross nodded regretfully and leaned forward to crush his cigarillo in the ashtray.

'With that sort of background, he probably did. I think honest people don't try to exploit others. I think you gain most loyalty from any employee if you treat him fairly. Usually that means less profit, and unfortunately most bosses are only concerned with the size of their profit.'

His voice was soothing. He was someone who knew what he was talking about. She felt relaxed and at home with him.

'What do you trade in?' she asked.

'Optical and nautical apparatus. My brother and I are partners. Until now we were just based in Singapore, but Hong Kong is becoming an important location and we decided to open a subsidiary there.

'When I return I intend to live in Hong Kong and establish a main office. I bought a plot of ground in an auction before I left, and my house is in construction at this moment. Our trade with China increases constantly so Hong Kong is ideal, geographically and politically. The presence of the British military on the island gives us the safe haven and protection we need to operate without hostility.' He brushed any stray ash from his silk waistcoat.

'Anyway . . . Why aren't you in the drawing-room with all the other ladies? I stayed here because I wanted to finish

18

my cigarillo in peace.' He could see her interest was genuine, and Ross couldn't remember when he had last had such a normal, unstilted conversation with a woman, or talked to a woman about his business.

'No-one will miss me. I often disappear when my uncle and aunt have visitors. I just came down to get this book.' She reached forward and picked one up from the desk. 'I left it here this morning.'

'What is it about? A Gothic mystery? Women seem to be reading them all the time nowadays.'

'I read them, too, now and then, because they are entertaining, but this book is by someone who disputes Darwin's 'The Origin of Species'.'

His brows raised and there was complete surprise on his face.

'And you think that it's worth reading?'

'Yes. This particular author disputes Darwin's conclusions but I think Mr Darwin is probably right. He gathered a great deal of information about all kinds of plants and animals in their natural habitats, and sailed around the world comparing similar species in different situations.

'His findings and conclusions are logical. He's not the first scientist who suggested this theory. Other scientists have advocated the same thing before, but they never went into such detail or were able to itemise their justifications.'

He got up. Sarah looked up into his dark eyes.

Her words intrigued him. She was a very unusual woman. She was wasted, hidden away like this.

'Many others, the church in particular, is still up in arms, and it's been ten years since Darwin published his findings,' he remarked.

'I know — but anyone who presents a new idea is often treated with scorn. I want to read what this man thinks is so wrong about Darwin's ideas. It is a thin book; it will not take me long to finish.'

He moved closer and viewed her

more closely. There was both delicacy and strength in her face.

'Does your uncle approve of you reading such things?'

She studied his face. Instinctively she felt could say anything she liked to him.

'Good heavens, no, Mr Balfour! In his opinion, women should be seen and not heard. I use my spare time to read. No-one knows. If they did, he would forbid me to do so and tell me to spend more time with my Bible. I hope they think I'm reading religious commentaries or something equally boring.'

He laughed and his brilliant eyes twinkled. He also felt an inkling of pleasure that she seemed to know that he would not reveal her secret to anyone else.

'Well, I won't tell on you, I promise! I think I must join the others now, before someone comes looking for me.'

She smiled at him and he thought what a refreshing young woman she was. She had a genial face, made sensible comments, the colour of her hair was fantastic, and her lips were full and rounded over even teeth.

'Yes, I'll disappear upstairs again too. Goodnight, Mr Balfour. It was a pleasure to meet you.'

He dipped his head.

'Likewise! Goodnight, Miss Courtney.' He turned on his heel and strode to the door, leaving it open behind him.

On her way to her room, Sarah regretted that she would probably never converse with him so intimately again. Perhaps they would never meet again. He was courteous, and not patronising — an interesting man who listened and hadn't dismissed her words as nonsense. He didn't mind her candour, either.

She guessed that most of the businessmen who dealt with her uncle would have been appalled if she any spoken so openly to them. That was why she disliked attending the dinner parties so much. She found it impossible to restrict her dialogue to the weather, church matters, coming social events, the paintings on the walls, or the Royal Family.

★ ★ ★

Next morning, Sarah's aunt declared the evening had been a great success. Her uncle had won a new contract for potato sacks, and Ross Balfour had promised to call again.

Sarah nodded, pleased when she heard his name, and continued to busy herself with repairing some loose flounces on one of Abigail's dresses. She preferred to be occupied than to sit around staring into space or reading religious sermons, and Abigail hated sewing.

Sometimes Sarah ran errands for her aunt if the maid was employed elsewhere, and she always enjoyed those short times of freedom. Generally, she went alone, because no other servant was free to accompany her.

Sarah was grateful that the whole family had never shown any hostility that she had been foisted on them. She tried to show her appreciation by making herself useful.

Abigail, wasn't hostile, either. Someone had to care for Sarah and her parents decided it was their duty. In fact, having Sarah in the house was very useful, because now Sarah often did Abigail's chores, giving Abigail more time for studying fashion magazines, taking dancing lessons, going on picnics and attending other entertainments with friends.

In the beginning Sarah had gone with Abigail, but found most of the excursions were extremely boring and silly. Sarah also thought most of the young people were harebrained and honestly declared she wasn't interested in such pastimes.

Her aunt warned her she was not likely to attract a suitable husband if she did not join in. Sarah countered she was not likely to attract anyone of any status anyway, and she wasn't looking. She was happy being useful to her aunt.

She proved herself to be competent as well as useful. Thankfully, her aunt soon dropped the idea of encouraging her to go to social gatherings.

Her aunt and uncle were steady churchgoers, staunch believers, and they believed caring for Sarah was their duty and their religious responsibility.

Sarah concluded that her new guardians would never force her into marrying anyone unless her uncle went bankrupt.

Sarah had only once asked if her uncle would allow her to use the money from the sale of her father's shop to buy a small cottage and live there peacefully with a companion. Her uncle brushed his grey side whiskers with his fingers, looked briefly at his gold pocket-watch, and then folded both hands behind his back. He frowned, and shook his head.

'That is an extremely silly idea, Sarah. You are much too young to live on your own, and what would you do with your time? Here you are useful and can help your aunt. One day, when you are much older and still not married, we will perhaps talk of this again, but you know very well that I don't approve of you, or any other woman, living on her own.'

No Place for a Woman

The weather remained inclement and Abigail filled her time visiting, or being visited. She invited Sarah along, but Sarah sidestepped the invitations. She avoided going out in the cold and mist whenever she could. Staying home was more pleasant.

'I think Paul has his eye on you,' Abigail mentioned once. 'He always asks where you are, and why you don't join us.'

'Does he? Tell him that I've a secret admirer in Leicester, and that I'm pining for him. That will put him off. He's personable, but not my idea of an ideal companion.'

Abigail looked thoughtful.

'Isn't he? I think he's nice. He'll take over his father's bank one day, and he's solid, respectable, and dutiful. He never misses a Sunday church service, either.'

Sarah didn't reply, but it was just those qualities that made her uneasy.

One afternoon Aunt Sybil received an urgent message for her husband. Their maid was already out on another errand so her aunt thrust the envelope into Sarah's hand.

'You'll have to deliver it to him at his office, Sarah. Hurry, and don't talk to anyone else on the way there or back.'

The company offices were near the town centre. Sarah set off. She didn't want a soggy and scruffy skirt so she lifted it so that it did not drag on the wet pavements. She didn't have many replacements.

When she reached the red-bricked offices, and their adjoining warehouse, the man in charge there recognised her.

'Are you looking for Mr Courtney, ma'am?'

'Yes, I have an urgent message for him.'

'He's gone down to the waterfront. A

ship we were waiting for docked this morning and he's checking the cargo, before it's sent to the factory.'

She nodded.

'Thank you. Do you know the name of the ship?'

'*Windswept*, ma'am. I hope you are not thinking of going there? The waterfront is no place for a lady.'

She smiled.

'I've been there before. It's all right.'

He scratched his head and looked unconvinced.

'I bet you've not been there on your own though, have you? It's getting dark. I would deliver it for you if I could, but I dare not leave the warehouse unattended.'

'Oh, don't worry about me. I'll be all right. It's still early. I'll hurry there and back. It's not far.'

'Well, be very careful, miss, and don't talk to anyone. There are a lot of rough people living in that part of the town. Dock workers and all kinds of hangers-on.'

'I'll take care. Thank you. I'll deliver my message and hurry home again, promise!' She smiled at him and set off.

With her head down, Sarah held on to her hat. It was now spotting rain and the wind was blustery. Her woollen cape was soon clammy. She gave up trying to save the hem of her skirt and the petticoats underneath from the wet and the mud.

The nearer she got to the waterfront, the messier and dirtier the pavements became. The afternoon light was fading fast, but she reckoned she could still get to the docks and be back home again before darkness.

Gas lighting illuminated the main public thoroughfares in the town, but the less frequented streets like this one had no illumination. Should she turn back after all, and ask her aunt to send one of the servants?

She straightened her shoulders and carried on, passing neglected and unloved houses. Only an occasional person went by, going in the other direction, not looking at her as they hurried past.

After a few minutes of seeing no-one, two men approached, walking together side by side. They were clearly dock workers, rough and grubbily dressed. When they reached Sarah the two men blocked her way and grinned at her.

Sarah looked down, rounded her shoulders and tried to pass them on the inside of the pavement, but they stood their ground, and blocked her path. Sarah stepped back.

The taller of the two had a soiled kerchief around his neck and a ragged flat cap that had seen much better days.

'Well, well! And what's a fancy little bird like you doing in this part of town?'

'It's none of your business. Let me pass, fellow!' she replied, trying not to show her apprehension.

He stuck his hands in his pockets and leered. One of his front teeth was missing.

'Why should I? Perhaps you're

31

looking for protection?'

'No, I'm not. Why don't you just get out of my way?'

He grinned.

'Haven't you heard about the young girls who ended up in dire straits after walking around this area on their own? With companions like my friend and myself you would be safe. Where are you going?'

Sarah could barely understand his broad accent.

'Mind your own business and just leave me alone,' she repeated, feeling hot and uneasy.

His companion started to chuckle. The first man reached out his dirty hand towards her. She knocked his arm away and stepped out on to the road to pass them. He attempted to make another grab for her, but a walking stick swished through the air on to the man's arm. He yelped.

'What the . . . ' His voice trailed away when he saw his antagonist was a bigger man, someone whose rich clothing told him that he came from better circles.

The man's deep voice was threatening.

'You've both annoyed this lady long enough. You both deserve a thrashing and if you don't move off, I'll show you exactly what I think of you, and your behaviour.'

Somehow the man's voice was familiar to Sarah, but his features were hidden in the shadows.

'No offence intended, sir,' the worker blustered. 'My friend and I are respectable labourers. We were only having a little fun.' The two men stood side by side facing him. Inches separated them. The stranger held his walking-stick in a menacing grip, and the man and his friend backed off.

'Huh! And I can imagine the fun I'll have teaching you manners. You'd better leave now! Otherwise you'll both be sorry.'

The shorter of the two doffed his cloth cap.

'Come on, Harry, let's go. I ain't

clashing with the gentry. They stick together, and if I lose my job, my wife will kill me!'

Mumbling and with backward glances, the two hurried off into the darkness. Sarah felt relief and uttered.

'Thank you, sir. They were indeed bothering me.'

'Miss Courtney! What on earth are you doing in this part of the town on your own, at this time of day? Silliness is not the right word — it's sheer stupidity.'

Her pulse increased when she realised it was Ross Balfour.

Her Secret is Safe

'Mr Balfour! What a surprise.' He had moved close enough now for her to see him properly, and she could also tell by his expression that he was annoyed.

He glared at her.

'What in the devil's name are you doing here?'

Catching her breath, she explained briefly about delivering her message to her uncle.

'I'm sure your aunt would be shocked if she knew you had embarked on such a risky undertaking.'

She looked down.

'My aunt said it was urgent, and I honestly didn't think it was unsafe. It's not very far from my uncle's office to the wharf, and it was daylight when I set out. I've been to the dockside before.'

His voice was still sharp and critical.

'That may be so, but certainly not during the evening, or on your own! It was mere chance that I was walking on the opposite side of the road and saw those two louts troubling you.' He came closer and took her arm. 'I'll accompany you for the rest of the way.'

'Oh . . . please don't inconvenience yourself. I'll be fine now. I'll be there in a couple of minutes.'

Impatiently he ignored her remark.

'The men around the dockside, loading or unloading the ships, are not likely to be any better than the two you just met. My conscience will not allow me to leave you to walk on your own. I wish you had been more sensible and not set out on your own in the first place.'

Feeling annoyed by his high-handedness, Sarah fell in step with him and remained silent. A few minutes of avoiding muck and puddles, gave her time to think sensibly. She finally admitted he was right. She had misjudged the situation.

'I'm sorry if I've caused you any trouble,' she said quietly. 'You are right, I should not have come on my own. I should have let someone else deliver the message. I did think about going home, honestly, but decided to carry on, because I knew the way and didn't reckon with any danger.'

'In daylight, and in company, it would be an understandable decision,' he said, now sounding less threatening, 'but not on your own, and not at this time of the day.'

There was silence for a while as they strolled along. Then she heard him chuckle.

'If this is the way you behave generally, your aunt and uncle are probably having a very trying time.'

She stopped suddenly in her tracks and some drops of rain fell from the brim of her hat on to her cheek.

'I hope not,' she answered heatedly. 'I always try to be decorous, but on occasion, if the day is too humdrum, I do enjoy getting away for a while. I don't intentionally cause them any trouble, I just long for some variation and new experiences in my life sometimes. And I don't find it exciting to go to tea-parties, or attend soirées.'

He looked at her and tried to define her expression in the darkness. His anger faded away and he felt a growing sympathy.

'It sounds like you thirst for adventure.'

'Adventure is the wrong expression, but I do wish I could decide for myself. My father allowed me as much freedom as he could. My uncle and aunt have completely different standards, and I must learn to adjust.' She paused. 'I don't know why I'm telling you this. I hope you will not repeat it to anyone?'.

He touched the brim of his hat.

'No, your secrets are safe with me. One day, when you marry, things may change.'

They resumed their walk.

'I've no great dowry to attract

anyone,' she replied, 'and anyway I think I would be very unhappy unless I was treated as an equal. The vast majority of men I've met, want a docile, submissive wife. I'd be happy to live on my own and do something useful with my life. My father left enough money for me to do that, but my uncle says it is ridiculous for a woman like me to have such scatterbrained ideas.'

He laughed.

'Well, who knows. Perhaps you will fall in love with someone who understands your independent character and who will support you.'

She shook her head and the raindrops on the brim of her hat took flight.

'That is a daydream. I've decided that I'll probably end up as elderly companion to my aunt, and an unpaid nanny to my cousin's children.'

He chuckled.

'That is a very dreary prospect.'

She sighed.

'Yes, I know, but unless I suddenly inherit a huge fortune from someone unknown to me, that is what is going to happen.'

They had reached the harbour.

'Which ship?' he asked.

'*Windswept*. My uncle's manager said it is berthed on the far side of the dock.'

They passed several men who looked at them curiously, but no-one dared to speak to her when Ross was at her side.

When they reached the ship, her uncle was talking to the captain. His eyebrows lifted as they approached.

'Mr Balfour! And what on earth are you doing here, Sarah?'

Ross touched the brim of his hat.

'Your niece has an important message from your wife, and we met near your office. I offered to bring her here.'

'Hmm! Good thing you met her, sir. This is no place for a lady.' He held out his hand and Sarah reached into her pocket for the message. He moved underneath a nearby lantern to read the contents, and nodded to himself.

Sarah turned to Ross.

'Thank you . . . for not giving me away,' she whispered.

His eyes twinkled, and for some reason Sarah wished it was daylight and she could see their colour. She was now almost convinced that they were a murky green. Her uncle returned.

'Thank you, child. This will save me a lot of time. You will have to wait before we can go home, I'm afraid. You can make yourself comfortable in the cabin and I'll fetch you later.'

Ross intervened.

'Miss Courtney is wet from walking here. If your work is going to keep you, I suggest that I take her home now. There must be a carriage we can hire. It'll be no trouble.'

Her uncle hesitated for a moment but then he nodded.

'It is kind of you, Mr Balfour. Yes, you are right, she must get out of those wet clothes. Tell your aunt not to delay the meal, Sarah. I'll eat later. Wait here. I'll get one of the men to find you a carriage.'

Sarah felt delighted to know she was to have Ross's company for a little while longer.

Safe and Sound

During the journey, Sarah's clothes did feel damp and uncomfortable, but she didn't really care as she listened to Mr Balfour talking about Singapore. It sounded like paradise.

'It must be wonderful to see such things and be part of it all.'

He looked ahead.

'Yes, I suppose it is, but never forget there is a lot of poverty and misery, too. Europeans try to impose our culture on the local people. That is not good. We tend to think our ways, our methods, our intentions are best, but I don't always agree. Sometimes I think we do more damage than good.'

'Surely employment and new ideas do improve the lives of many of the poor?'

'The lowest levels of society are exploited by their own people as well as by us. We are there to do business, and most of us are planning to return home, rich and successful, one day.

'Just a small section of the local population profits from our presence and who knows what will happen when we leave. One day they will manage things on their own, but that is still far in the future. Until then, as long as we have control, we have the say.'

'You told me that you will live in Hong Kong? What does it look like?'

He chuckled.

'You are an inquisitive soul, aren't you? It is growing fast. It is a small island and things were much rougher the first time I went there some years ago. There is now a dedicated church, government buildings, and there are shops and entertainments.

'Society has already organised lots of things. Women have done a great deal to civilise it. Today they have their tea parties, meetings and enjoyments.

'You can't compare Hong Kong to a European city, but that is where it is heading. Its strategic position makes it an interesting base for military purposes. The European population is concentrated on one part of the island, the Chinese population makes do with the rest.

'While the Europeans watch cricket or enjoy horse racing, the Chinese live in the most deplorable hovels. This overcrowding, and awful conditions are reasons why there are constant outbreaks of fatal illnesses. The authorities try to keep things under control, but some illnesses spread at great speed and there is little anyone can do to stop it happening once it takes hold.

'Some places where the Chinese population settled was just swampland. The Chinese are still crowded together. You wouldn't believe how they put up with it, but they don't protest and seem to prefer living huddled together.

'Most of the time they have no other choice, because it is overcrowded everywhere and the Europeans decide where new settlements will be allowed, or not.'

To Sarah the journey went too fast and Ross felt flattered by the genuine interest she showed about his business and his lifestyle.

He helped her out of the carriage and when a servant opened the door, he waited on the steps with her. Tipping his hat, he was about to leave when Sarah's aunt hurried out to join them. She eyed Sarah briefly.

'Good heavens, child, you look like a drowned rat. Go and get changed at once. I don't want you ill on my hands.' She turned to Ross. 'Mr Balfour, how kind of you to bring Sarah home. Please come in and tell me what happened.' She turned to Sarah again and flicked her hands in the direction of the stairs. 'Off with you.'

Laying her hand on Ross's arm she directed him inside.

'Charles, pay the driver, and take Mr Balfour's hat and coat. Come, come,

Mr Balfour! You must tell us how it happens that you accompany Sarah home. Abigail is in the drawing-room and she will be delighted to see you.'

With a departing look at Sarah who was climbing the stairs, he gave in and handed his coat, hat, and silver-topped walking stick to the servant before following his hostess into the drawing-room. Mrs Courtney insisted he sat next to Abigail on the sofa facing a blazing fire in the grate.

'I'll order some tea. I'm sure you will welcome some hot refreshments on a night like this.' She hurried to the door and left him alone with Abigail.

Ross stayed as long as politeness allowed. Sarah did not reappear, as her aunt had sent a message with Masie to tell her she was not to reappear until her hair was dry and neatly arranged. Her hair took a long time to dry because the heat from the fire in her bedroom was not as lavish as the fires in some of the other rooms. When she decided she was presentable again,

47

she hurried downstairs only to find that Mr Balfour had left.

Her aunt looked pleased.

'It was a fortunate that you met Mr Balfour like that, Sarah. It meant that he could converse with Abigail. I invited him to dinner on Friday, and he accepted.'

Sarah was pleased that she might see him again soon, but was uneasy about the fact that her aunt had clearly picked him out for special attention. He was too intelligent, kind, and interesting to be the object of her aunt's ambitions.

She shrugged, and told herself it was none of her business. She was sure he was too self-confident to let anyone else push him into making any wrong decisions. She wondered if the need for European female company would colour his judgement.

She had read that many European men living and working in foreign regions often had native mistresses. Perhaps Ross Balfour had a mistress, too. On the other hand, he might be looking for a European bride — to share his official lifestyle. He could still have a mistress for pleasure. Perhaps he was beginning to think it was time to marry and have children.

She took her embroidery out of the drawer of a side-table and began to work on it. Her aunt cut in on her thoughts.

'Mr Balfour told us what happened. It was not wise of you to walk to the wharf just because your uncle was not in his office. If Mr Balfour had not offered to accompany you, anything could have happened. You should have sent someone else with the message.'

Sarah looked up.

'There was no-one else in the office I could send. The manager had to safeguard the warehouse and the office. I thought the message was exceedingly important, so I was grateful to meet Mr Balfour and accept his company.

'Did he mention that uncle told me to tell you not to hold supper? He is still busy and does not know what time he will be home.' She searched frantically in her pocket for a handker-chief and sneezed.

'There!' Abigail declared, sounding triumphant. 'That is what you get when you act foolishly. Now you have caught a cold.'

Sarah continued plying her needle.

'But I delivered the message. Just because I sneeze does not mean that I've caught a cold.'

But she had.

A Precious Gift

Sarah's cold got worse, and her aunt called the doctor who declared she must keep to her bed and take his medicine until her chest was clear. After he left, Sarah declared she could mix a better medication herself. Standing next to her, her aunt laughed and shook her head.

On Friday morning she felt much better and looked forward to the evening, mainly because Ross was coming. She looked down quickly in dismay when her aunt declared that she was still not well enough to join their guests.

'Anyway, I didn't think you would be fit enough when I planned the evening. If you joined now, there would be thirteen. I can't set a dinner table for thirteen people; it would be very unlucky.'

Her happy anticipation faded as her aunt bustled about her room tidying things.

'You can still be very useful, Sarah,' her aunt said, wanting to soothe any disappointment. 'Will you help Abigail to look her best? You can often persuade her where I cannot. She talks of side curls, but with her round face it does not suit her. A roll becomes her much better.'

'Who is coming?' Sarah asked quietly.

'Canon Walters, Mr Wilson, and Lord Ellesporte with their wives, Abigail has invited her friend Milly, then there's Mr Balfour, Paul Byatt and your uncle and me.' She lifted the watch pinned to her blouse.

'Dear me!' she exclaimed. 'I've forgotten to warn Bessie not to include any nuts in the menu. Apparently, Mrs Wilson is allergic. I hope it's not too late. It will be expensive to replace the venison and beef.' She scurried out.

Sarah sighed softly, and felt slightly

wretched. She wouldn't miss meeting any of the others, but for some reason she had been looking with pronounced pleasure to seeing Ross Balfour again. Would he notice her absence? Probably not. She picked up her book and concentrated on the contents.

In the evening she helped Abigail form a thick roll of her hair and threaded some florets of roses along its length. It looked very stylish.

Sarah settled in the bedroom's comfortable armchair with a book, tried to concentrate and read until she felt tired. She went along the corridor to the bathroom and heard someone playing the piano and laughter from down below. She hurried to shut the door.

Her uncle was extremely proud of their bathroom. It was one of the most modern money could buy, and Sarah admitted it was luxury in comparison to her father's home where the toilet was outside, and they had a sink and a tin bath.

Papa put any profit he made into

improving the shop or investing in new treatments and medications.

She smiled as she got ready for the night. She recalled Papa's intelligent eyes twinkling behind his spectacles as he tried to explain where all the money had gone.

She fell asleep and slept better than she expected. She was always one of the first down to breakfast every morning. The years with her father had taught her how precious the first hours of the day could be, when there was no-one else around.

She went to the breakfast-room and a few minutes later Charles, the butler, followed her with a pot of tea in one hand, and a small brown parcel and note in the other. He handed them to her.

'Mr Balfour requested me to give them to you this morning with the note, miss.'

Her pulse jumped and she felt end-lessly pleased that he had not forgotten her.

'Thank you, Charles.' She had never been more pleased that she was alone. She waited until he had closed the door and opened the note.

'Dear Miss Courtney,

I was sorry not to have your company this evening, and I hope you will soon be feeling much better. I hope the included items will help to banish any boredom you may feel during the time you are on the way to recovery, and not yet well enough for your normal undertakings (such as walking in places where you should not be walking!) The one book will interest your intellect, the other will stir your fantasy. I hope they both give you pleasure.

I've tagged behind in the library, like last time we met, to find pen and paper! I'm leaving Dundee, as I've promised to spend some time with a cousin who owns a small estate near Pitlochry. I know the area well, and am looking forward to some bracing, uplifting walks (if it stops raining long enough).

The mountain scenery is perfect for someone like myself who enjoys an invigorating walk but not the challenge of the formidable elevations of the Cairngorms.

Wishing you a speedy recovery.

Ross Balfour.'

She stared at his sturdy writing and thought what a kind and generous man he was. He barely knew her.

She ripped away the brown paper. There were two books. One was entitled 'The Variations Of Animals And Plants Under Domestication' by Charles Darwin, and the other was '20,000 Leagues Under The Sea' by Jules Verne. She glanced at the first pages of both and then held them to her chest in delight.

When she heard her uncle's steps she quickly stuck the note in the pocket of her dress, bunched the books and the paper together and shoved them under the table where she could reclaim them at leisure.

'Good morning, Sarah. You're looking much better this morning. Good! Good!'

She smiled at him.

'Yes, I feel fine. A busy day today?'

There was nothing her uncle enjoyed more than talking about his business and how much hard work he faced in the coming day. Sarah listened with half an ear and hoped she nodded at the right moment.

She was disappointed that she wouldn't have the chance to thank Ross Balfour for his kindness and, with her thoughts centred on him, she still recall his features very clearly.

During the course of the day, neither her aunt or Abigail mentioned a gift of books so Sarah didn't, either. They were small enough to have fitted in the capacious pocket of his evening coat.

Perhaps someone had mentioned she was ill when he arrived, and he had retrieved them later, adding the note before he left.

★ ★ ★

The days and weeks passed. The weather was dismal and although her aunt never admitted it, she was disappointed that Ross Balfour had not shown any special interest in Abigail.

'He is a very presentable young man,' she remarked to Sarah one day. 'Ambitious, clever and already rich. Perhaps he'll call again before he leaves for China. I hope so. He did say that he was planning to leave in early summer, so he will be around for a couple of months yet. I believe he is visiting some relatives at present.'

Bending over some mending, Sarah had to stop herself blurting out that he was staying in Pitlochry with his cousin. She bit her lip and said nothing.

Aunt Sybil straightened her shoulders.

'But . . . Paul Byatt left his calling

card twice since the last time he was here. He is also a very presentable young man. His father owns the bank in Culloden Street. Abigail was out with Milly when he came, both times. It's a pity. I was hoping he would call again.'

Sarah nodded.

'Does Abigail like him?' Sarah found Paul flat company in comparison to Ross Balfour. Why was she comparing other men to him? It was a silly habit. 'Abigail told me she met Paul when she went to that soirée last week. He danced with her a couple of times.'

Her aunt's eyes brightened.

'Did he? Abigail didn't tell me that. She's a silly girl sometimes. I must find a way to gain his interest. Can you think of something? There's no point in encouraging him unless it is done in a socially appropriate way.'

'Why don't you ask him if he has time to accompany you both on a visit to the theatre? Tell him Uncle Aidan can't come. You could invite him for a meal beforehand. I expect he'd be flattered.'

Her aunt studied the row of silver-framed family photos on the long dark sideboard and adjusted the position of one.

'Yes, we could do that. We would be with others in the theatre and I could sit at the back of the box. A meal here with your uncle beforehand would be quite in order. Yes, it's not a bad idea. I'll talk it over with Grace and see what she thinks.'

She stood up and hurried to the door.

'I'll send her a note to ask her to come around this afternoon.'

Grace was her aunt's best friend and a guru when it came to what was correct behaviour. Sarah was glad. It meant she would have a free afternoon. Abigail was planning to go shopping for a new bonnet with Milly.

★   ★   ★

They celebrated Christmas in a rich and traditional way. Abigail loved every moment and even spent time making cards to send to people Sarah had never heard of, and searching for suitable presents for her parents and Sarah.

She gave Sarah a pair of warm gloves that were very welcome, and Sarah gave Abigail a self-made netted silver-thread purse. Sarah recalled nostalgically how she and Papa had enjoyed a much quieter time together, without presents.

On Boxing Day, the house was full of noise, with young people coming and going, neighbours and friends calling, and even some distant relations arriving who declared they didn't even know that Sarah's father had passed away. Some stayed overnight, and when everyone left, Sarah sighed with relief.

When people, declared Hogmanay was even more important, she wished she could disappear and come back when it was all over.

Abigail loved the whole season and her aunt was delighted that Paul seemed enamoured of her daughter and had even chosen her as his partner when a group of young people went first-footing.

Listening to the bells announcing 1870, Sarah sat at the open window of her small room with her hand on Ross's books. Was he was celebrating somewhere at this moment?

A Suitable Match

January and February were dismal months and Abigail and her mother were troubled by heavy colds. In Aunt Sybil's case, it developed into bronchitis and that meant that the running of the household fell to Sarah. She didn't mind because it helped to fill her days.

Her uncle complained that the storms in the North Sea were delaying ships bringing the raw jute and the factory reserves were considerably reduced. His ships were still using the route around the. Cape of Good Hope.

The Suez Canal had been opened a few months earlier and reports in the newspapers stated how it significantly shortened the journey east to west, or west to east.

Uncle Aidan remarked he would still

use the old route because, at present, it was still cheaper for transporting bulk goods.

Abigail made no objection that Sarah was running the household for her mother. She was content to join the circle of her friends again. They met to play cards, drink hot chocolate and gossip about the friends who weren't present. She even invited her friends to tea-parties at home, and asked Sarah to organise the teas.

Sarah wondered how she would manage when she had a home of her own. Perhaps she would be more interested in such things when that happened?

Attending the service every week in St Paul's Chapel was a must. The only acceptable excuse for not going was if someone was ill. As long as it was fine, they walked to the large church and all the other families they knew did so, too.

As Sarah sat on one of the hard, wooden benches and stared up at the long stained-glassed windows, she listened with growing reluctance to the minister, who regularly declared hell and damnation on anyone who was not living the kind of moral and religious life he defined as desirable.

Sarah preferred to spend her time thinking about things like Darwin's theory — and why the church was so incensed when he suggested man was descended from the apes.

She liked to believe that God was a lot more compassionate towards sinners and offenders than the man in the pulpit told them he was. His voice rang out and echoed as he ranted and raved about the dangers of waywardness amongst his parishioners, but he failed to condemn real injustices like poverty and repression in the world in general.

One Sunday at the end of February after the service, her aunt and Abigail were gossiping with friends and Sarah was standing next to her uncle when Paul Byatt joined them. He tipped his hat briefly to her and began to talk to Sarah's uncle.

Sarah listened with half an ear because the two men began to discuss business. Paul was deputy in his father's bank, so the state of trade and industry was of paramount importance to them both and that was the centre of their discussions.

Sarah's attention was wakened when she heard Ross Balfour's name mentioned.

'A very clever businessman,' Paul said stiffly, 'but he is not the kind of man I'd choose as a friend. He is too tight-lipped. I think there is something uncanny about someone who chooses to do business in outlandish places.

'I met him briefly in London at a social gathering. He said he had just negotiated a favourable deal with a manufacturer of specialist lenses. He is still visiting some other firms who produce parts for his various optical apparatus.

'He was there as the guest of the

owner of a firm on the Welsh border and who has another factory in Norwich.'

Her uncle viewed him sympathetically.

'You must admit that he's a canny entrepreneur, Paul. You can't blame him for that, and we need people who are prepared to go abroad to trade.

'Balfour must like it wherever he lives at present, because rumour has it that he doesn't need to go back. He has made enough money to remain here enjoying a splendid time for the rest of his life.'

'Our country is the centre of industry and commerce,' Paul retorted doggedly. 'What he trades in is not so important.'

Sarah stared steadfastly ahead and held her tongue.

'Our colonies are a source of great wealth, Paul,' her uncle replied steadily, 'and you must remember that trade flows in both directions. We need these outposts of the British Empire for raw materials and cheap labour. My own business depends on raw jute. It is cheapest from Bangladesh.

'A lot of materials for our other industries come from abroad, and we sell our finished products to customers at home and abroad. Continued expansion encourages manufacturers to develop new products, use new methods, and these in turn bring us even greater profits. Balfour's products are sought after, otherwise he wouldn't be successful.'

Fiddling with the silver top of his cane, and agreeing reluctantly, Paul nodded.

'Perhaps you are right. By the way, he asked me to remember him to your family.'

'Did he now! Is he coming back to Dundee?'

'He didn't actually say so. We only spoke for a couple of minutes, but I did get the impression it was a possibility because he asked how everyone was, and seemed interested in hearing what has been going on since he left.'

'My wife will be pleased to hear that,' her uncle answered, unenlightened that Paul had been seeing a lot of Abigail in recent times. 'I think she was hoping Balfour would show special interest in our girl.'

'Pah! He doesn't deserve Abigail, sir. She's too good for the likes of Ross Balfour.'

Sarah itched to retort that Ross Balfour was too good for Abigail. She also knew she wouldn't. Her uncle would disapprove of any forwardness and would remonstrate with her later if she did, so she remained silent.

That evening as they ate their meal, which was less elaborate on Sunday because it was the servants' day off, her uncle told them that Balfour wished to be remembered. Her aunt's face brightened noticeably.

'That was good of him, don't you agree, Abigail? It will be extremely pleasing to see him again.' She turned to her husband. 'If you hear that Mr Balfour is back in Dundee, and you

69

happen to meet him, tell him he is always welcome to share an evening meal with us.'

Chuckling softly to himself, he nodded.

'Of course, my dear, if that is what you wish. Business contacts are always welcome.'

A Wish Come True

March arrived, the temperatures were milder and there was less rain. It was still cool, but Sarah enjoyed the freshness of the wind and being able to walk outside without feeling frozen to the bone.

She retained the hope that Ross Balfour would come back, and she would see him again. It seemed as though her wish might be realised when her uncle made an announcement one day.

'I met Balfour yesterday, we talked about business for a few minutes, and then I remembered your comments and I invited him to dinner. He responded positively and said any evening next week would be suitable, so I suggested Thursday.'

His wife beamed.

'That's very pleasing, my dear. We must try to make up a fitting company, and I'll speak with the cook tomorrow so that we have a memorable meal.' She turned to Abigail. 'It's very apt that the new evening gown you ordered will be finished this week, isn't it?'

'Another dress? The girl has too many already. You're making too much fuss, my dear.'

'Ah, but Abigail must make an impression, and this new dress is of a fantastic blue silk. It suits her perfectly.'

Uncle Aidan went on with his meal and remained silent as his wife and Abigail began to discuss fashions and accessories.

Sarah didn't mind helping to make Thursday evening perfect. There was nothing to stop her attending this time.

When Ross arrived, he looked extremely handsome and at ease in the correctness of his black and white evening dress. When they met, he touched her gloved hand briefly, his eyes twinkling.

'How delightful to meet you again, Miss Courtney. You were indisposed last time I was here.'

She reddened.

'Yes, sir. It is good to see you again.'

His white teeth flashed.

'How kind of you to say so.'

There was no further conversation because her aunt ushered him along to meet the other guests.

The meal went well and conversation flowed easily. Ross commented rarely, and only if he had something pertinent to say. He clearly didn't believe in talking for the sake of presenting himself like some of the other men.

Abigail was next to him again. Her new dress did suit her fair colouring. The elaborately draped overskirt and its bustle was festooned with tiny blue flowers and she wore mid-length gloves, that were just coming into fashion.

Sarah wore the same dark green dress she wore last time. She didn't mind.

No-one would notice what she wore then or now. It was simpler in style with a close-fitting bodice, a square neck, and a sparingly draped skirt.

After the, meal, she went into the drawing-room with the ladies, while the men shared whisky and cognac in the library. When the gentlemen joined the ladies, Sarah served coffee at one of the side tables. Ross was the last to be served, and he remained standing next to her.

'How are you? Are you still reading unsuitable books?'

She looked into his twinkling eyes and smiled.

'You can hardly accuse me of reading unsuitable books when you supplied me with some. Thank you, they were both wonderful for different reasons. I would have written to thank you, but I didn't have an address. Did you enjoy your visit to your relatives?'

He nodded.

'Too cold, but there were wonderful walks around the hills. The stillness and beauty are something I miss sometimes when I'm in more tropical climes.'

She offered him more coffee and he refused.

'You have also been to London since we last met, I believe?' she asked. His dark brows lifted and he looked interested. 'Paul told my uncle he saw you there.'

'Paul? Oh, yes. I met him and we spoke quite briefly. London is too large, too busy and too tiring. I went to visit some manufacturers.'

'And you were successful?'

He chortled.

'Yes, I suppose I was. What have you been doing since that evening you were putting your life in danger by going to places you shouldn't go?'

She lifted her chin defiantly.

'I was not putting my life in danger, and I haven't done anything important since then. My life runs in quiet courses.'

'Tut! Tut! From what you told me, I expected you do something unethical.'

'Like what? A woman is always restricted, and whoever male is in charge decides what happens or not. In my case my uncle is responsible and he believes I should be contented enough, and satisfied with my life.'

He looked thoughtful.

'And what would you like to do?'

'To be independent and do something worthwhile.'

Her aunt bustled up.

'Sarah, you must not engage too much of Mr Balfour's attention. Come, Mr Balfour, I'd like you to meet my friend Grace Seymour. Abigail has agreed to sing for us in a moment, and I'm sure we'll enjoy that. She has a sweet voice, doesn't she, Sarah?'

Sarah nodded. Abigail could play the piano quite well and her voice, although untrained, was also very pleasant.

Ross nodded briefly in Sarah's direction, put his coffee cup on the table and followed her aunt. Sarah began discreetly to collect the empty cups on a silver tray and carried them back to the kitchen.

When she returned, the sound of Scottish folk songs and other popular music was in full swing. Ross was in one of the corners and his eyes were on Abigail playing the piano.

Sarah felt a twinge of envy, but was pleased that she had spoken to him for a few minutes. He seemed as comfortable in her company as she felt in his.

She viewed the whole company in the glow of a multitude of candles for a couple of minutes before she decided to slip away. She had borrowed a book from the lending library yesterday and it was beckoning her.

It was not likely Ross Balfour would have an opportunity to speak to her again, and he was the only interesting person present to whom she wanted to talk. Her dress swished as she quietly left the room.

She didn't see that soon after, Ross Balfour's gaze had travelled the room and became less animated when he didn't find what he was looking for.

* * *

Next morning they were sorting out what needed to be laundered that week.

'Mr Balfour has invited us to a picnic excursion next week,' her aunt said animatedly. 'He suggested we visit Broughty Castle. It's a pleasant trip in the carriage if the weather is fine. It is a little early in the year and it will not be very warm, but as long as we are dressed properly, it will be delightful.

'He says he will arrange for the picnic food and we can eat it in the shelter of the castle walls.'

Her aunt was busy sorting the serviettes from the previous evening.

'Oh, dear, someone has ruined this one with red wine. I hope it can be saved. Red wine is so difficult to remove. By the way, Sarah, if you do not wish to come, just say so. I know you do not always enjoy large companies. I think Mr Balfour is inviting all the people who have given him hospitality during his stay.'

Sarah hurried to reply.

'I would love to come. You know how much I like being out in the fresh air. As long as there is room in the carriage for me, of course,' she added quickly.

Her aunt patted her cheek.

'Of course you can come, my dear. You deserve an outing, and you are in the house too much. It is a pity that you do not like house parties and visiting like Abigail does, then you would meet a lot more people.'

Sarah smiled.

'I don't need continual company, Aunt. You know that. I was not used to constant society and entertainments when I lived with my parents. That has shaped my view of the world. I know that Abigail loves such things and that is perfectly in order. We are all different.'

Her aunt considered her for a moment.

'You are too pretty to waste the best years of your life, Sarah.'

Sarah laughed.

'I'm not wasting anything. I like my life as it is and I hope I'm making myself useful to you. I realise that you did not need to take me when father died. It was kind of you and my uncle.'

'It was our duty, Sarah,' her aunt said quietly, slightly embarrassed by such words, 'and you have been a good girl. No trouble at all.' She stood up. 'I must find out if the cook is making good use of the leftovers. Perhaps you will finish the sorting?'

'Yes, of course.'

Not as it Seems . . .

The following Friday afternoon a procession of carriages met on the outskirts of the town and drove to Broughty Ferry. Although the temperatures left much to be desired, the sun was shining and the wind was blowing crowds of fluffy clouds far above them in a blue sky.

Her uncle had taken one of his rare afternoons off from his work, and Sarah noticed there were many other businessmen and their families amongst the gathering on their arrival in Broughty Ferry. They gathered together at a spot overlooking the beach with its long, flat sands.

The view was stunning and Sarah longed to run along its length barefoot, but there was little chance of her ever doing that.

The group split into bunches strolling here and there and along the turfed surface overlooking the beach. Her gaze wandered among those present and she picked Ross out easily because he was taller than most of the men surrounding him.

She also noted the presence of some of Abigail's friends. Sarah walked alongside her aunt and uncle decorously for a while. Once they began lengthy exchanges with their acquaintances, Sarah touched her aunt's arm.

'I'm going to visit the castle, Aunt,' she said quietly.

'All right, my dear, but don't do anything silly. The servants are already arranging the tables for the food. Don't stay too long.'

'I won't.' Relishing in the freedom to do as she wished on her own, she set off to examine the castle. Some parts of it were in ruins, but other parts were still quite intact. She'd read that it belonged to the Duke of Argyle, but at present it didn't look like the kind of place any duke would choose as a permanent residence.

Not many others from the party seemed interested in the castle, so she soon found herself on her own. The wind grabbed at her cape and she tightened her hat's ribbons as she neared the bordering low railings overlooking the Tay river and the mouth of Firth of Tay far below. The sound of someone behind her surprised her.

'It's a superb view from here, isn't it?'

She turned. Her cheeks were already reddened by the wind and the colour increased when she faced Ross.

'Yes, It's wonderful. It's easy to understand why someone built a castle here. It overlooks the Firth. Anyone oncoming, friend or enemy, could be seen well in advance from up here.' She turned her attention to the scene down below again. 'Do you know what that is?' She pointed.

He came closer and looked down.

'That's the railway ferry. It crosses the Tay, and links the Aberdeen to

Edinburgh railway. I'll be on it soon, on my way to Manchester.'

She didn't like to think of him leaving.

'And then from there you go on board ship to Hong Kong?'

'Yes, I've finalised my business. I'll take leave of a couple of distant relatives in the next week or two, finish the shopping list my sister-in-law gave me, and then there is nothing more to keep me here.'

She nodded, bit her lip, and paused a second.

'When will you be coming back?'

He shrugged.

'Not for a year or two, unless some kind of breathtaking new technology emerges, and we need it for our products.'

The wind was playing havoc with his hair and his coat, but he reminded Sarah of a rock in the storm. She was convinced that he was not the kind of man who could be forced to do anything. His eyes twinkled.

'Perhaps next time we meet, you will be a staid housewife with a couple of children.'

She shook her head, and the animation left her face. She did not answer. The knowledge that he was leaving and she might never see him again almost robbed her of all pleasure in speaking to him now. There had been very few people in her life with whom she felt completely at ease. Ross Balfour was one of them.

He held out his elbow.

'I came looking for you because your aunt was worried you had fallen down somewhere and I volunteered to look for you. The others are gathering for the meal.'

'How silly of her to worry! As if I'm not capable of looking after myself.' She turned suddenly and a gust of wind lifted the fine wool of her dove-grey skirt and entangled it around one of the knobbed wrought-iron posts, that were set at intervals along the railings. She automatically pulled at the skirt.

She watched in horror as it ripped from top to bottom along one of the seams. The two bits blew haphazardly back and forth in the squally wind. She looked at the damage in a state of mute astonishment.

Ross grinned and started to laugh. He had to remind himself it was a disconcerting situation for her and he turned away to give her time to recover.

'Stop laughing, stop fooling around, and do something,' she ordered him fiercely.

Turning back to face her, his face was still full of amusement and he had to clear his voice before he spoke.

'What exactly do you want me to do?'

'I don't know. Something! Anything! My aunt will never forgive me. I can't go back to all the others looking like this.'

Underneath the torn skirt, her petticoat was on display, and the blustery wind also provided occasional brief glimpses of her wide-legged drawers.

She had barely finished bickering with him when another gust of wind caught the fluttering folds of her white petticoat and wrapped it around the same post. She was imprisoned and tried frantically to escape before more damage took place.

Wrestling with the material and wondering how to free her petticoat without displaying more of her underwear, she toppled and lost her balance. Ross lunged and grabbed her around her waist. Their combined weight dragged the entangled material from the post and ripped it, too. Sarah fell down and he fell on top of her.

She looked up into his green eyes and was lost in her reflections for a second. His jaw clenched and his eyes narrowed. Both of them recovered quickly and tried to free themselves.

Just as Ross was struggling to his feet, they noticed Uncle Aidan had been watching them. They had no idea how long he'd been there but his expression was ominous. He waited stiffly with his hands locked behind his back as they scrambled to their feet. Sarah coloured and tightened her grip on her tattered attire. Ross picked up his hat and straightened his coat.

'What in heaven's name is going on, Balfour?' Uncle Aidan thundered. 'What does this mean?'

A dishevelled nervous Sarah stood, feeling flustered, next to Ross.

'Uncle Aidan, there's a simple explanation.'

Her uncle lifted his hand.

'Stop! Young lady, I'll hear nothing about this from you. Make yourself decently presentable. Balfour, come with me.' He strode off and waited for Ross under the shadows of one of the nearby rough walls. Ross gave her a fleeting glance and then followed him.

While Sarah was trying to gather the ripped material and knotting it into some kind of concealment, the two men conversed, their voices varying in their intensity. Sarah brushed her windswept hair out of her face and waited until her uncle returned, with Ross in his wake.

'So, we have decided that Mr Balfour will take you back to our carriage and tell our driver to take you home, and then he is to return for your aunt, Abigail, and me. You will go with Mr Balfour around the back of the castle buildings now. You are not likely to meet anyone from our party there.

'I'll tell your aunt that you have a headache and Mr Balfour is taking you to the carriage and will then come back to his guests. He will visit me tomorrow and we will settle the rest.'

Confused by his final words, Sarah met his glance. Her face was pale, but her expression was resolute.

'What rest? What do you mean, Uncle? It was an innocent accident. Mr Balfour was only trying to help. The wind . . . '

Aidan Courtney lifted his hand and his expression was as stern as ever. Clearly, Ross hadn't been able to convince him it was a perfectly harmless situation.

'Sarah, there is always a public hunger for gossip, and if anyone sees you in the condition you are in at this moment, and knew you were in Mr Balfour's company, it would be nothing short of a scandal. No-one will believe you were just struggling with damage from the wind, as Balfour insists was the case. You would be the target of tea-party talk for weeks and months. I'll not allow you to cause your aunt any personal grief or ill-standing in the community.'

Ross stood with his arms held stiffly at his side, his coat neatly buttoned and his hat at a nifty angle.

'Mr Balfour has agreed to do the honourable thing and we will talk of everything in detail tomorrow. Leave now and try to avoid meeting anyone else at all costs.'

'But Uncle . . . ' Sarah's protests were smothered by Ross taking one of her arms and dragging her along, away from her uncle and his fierce expression. She had bunched dress material in her hand but her white petticoat still peeped through the gaps. He hurried her along.

'Mr Balfour, what did you and my uncle settle?' she hissed.

He spoke casually, as if the sentence was nothing remarkable, and not showing he was bothered.

'He was so incensed, the only way I could appease him was to say that I would offer for your hand.'

She stopped.

'You would what?' she squealed.

'Miss Courtney, your uncle caught us in a very compromising situation. To be honest, he is right. If the picnic party saw the state of your dress and heard that your uncle found us lying together on the ground, your reputation would be ruined for the rest of your life.'

'But . . . but why should you assent to a ridiculous agreement because of something that never happened? My uncle misjudged the situation and is unable to think straight at this moment. He will come to his senses. If I go home now no-one else will ever know what happened. You hardly know me and I'm sure you do not want me as your wife.'

He grinned.

'Perhaps not, but let us take one step at a time. We must now salvage the day, and I'll talk to your uncle tomorrow.' He paused for a second or two, as if thinking of something. 'In fact, I think it might even solve your dilemma.'

She struggled to speak.

'I do not want to be engaged, Mr Balfour. Marriage is not what I want from life.'

He tipped his head.

'I know that, but I'm just as sure that you do not want to live with society's disapproval for the rest of your life, either. Leave it up to me. Perhaps we can solve the problem more easily than you imagine.'

He tightened his grip on her elbow and Sarah had no choice but to follow him to the carriage. He helped her inside.

Sarah was still shocked and tried to curtail her growing outrage and fury. He noticed her expression, tilted his head and smiled. Unperturbed, he tipped his hat, nodded to the coachman, and strode away.

Her eyes were stony with anger as the carriage drove off. He was heading back to a group of picnickers who had no idea that Sarah Courtney's world had just been turned upside down.

Outrageous Proposal

Home again, Sarah hurried inside, pulling the tattered remnants of her dress and underwear together.

Luckily, no-one was in the hall and she sprinted upstairs to her room. She checked the damage with sadness. The rips in the skirt were too jagged to repair, but the bodice of the dress was still intact, and perhaps her aunt could give her enough matching material to make a new skirt. Her cotton underwear didn't matter. It could be easily repaired.

When the others returned in the late afternoon, Sarah decided to be downstairs. She glanced in a recent magazine on the table that was being published in Dundee since the previous year. She liked the title 'The People's Friend' and it seemed to have interesting contents.

Her aunt bustled into the drawing-room, followed by Abigail. They both removed their bonnets and sat down.

'Is your headache better, child?' her aunt asked. 'Such a pity. It was a pleasant afternoon wasn't it, Abigail?'

'Yes, Mother. It was rather windy, but there were plenty of places to shelter and it was fun to watch the men playing cricket on the beach. Everyone seems to have enjoyed themselves and the food was splendid.'

Her mother eyed her daughter's slim waist.

'Yes, but you must be careful, dear. Too much rich food and you'll have problems with your waistline before you're even married.'

'Yes, I know,' Abigail remarked, pouting. 'It's not fair. Men don't have to wear corsets but we do, because fashion demands it.'

Sarah joined in.

'Lots of portly men wear corsets. My father said so, and he said that it was not good for their digestive systems. One of our regular customers creaked when he came into the shop!'

Abigail laughed.

'Did he? Wasn't he embarrassed?'

Sarah shook her head.

'He was so used to it, I don't think he heard it himself. I wondered who laced him, because he was a bachelor.'

'Oh, probably his servant or the housekeeper.'

Mrs Courtney clapped her hands.

'Girls, that is quite enough! I think we can all agree to give the evening meal a miss.

Mr Courtney has gone to the docks. A new cargo was due to arrive this afternoon and he wanted to control the quality before it is unloaded.'

Abigail nodded and stood up.

'I'm going to Lottie Walters' tea party tomorrow. One of the flounces on my lemon dress needs repairing. Maisie will have to do it.' With her skirt and its bustle touching the door's framework, she left.

Sarah's aunt turned to Sarah.

'If you feel better, I expect you will settle down in a corner with a book like you always do. I'm going to lie down until your uncle returns.' She left, with her bonnet dangling from her hand.

Sarah gathered that her uncle had not yet told her aunt the real reason why she had left early. She wasn't looking forward to her aunt's reaction. She would be shocked, even though the whole thing had been perfectly innocent.

★   ★   ★

Next morning her aunt looked at her icily across the breakfast table, and no word was spoken. It was clear that her uncle had informed his wife, and Sarah was in disgrace.

Sarah decided to make herself scarce until the situation had settled. She escaped to her room and darned the thick winter socks that had accumulated in the basket in the laundry room.

She was there when Masie came to tell her the master wanted to talk to her. She hurried downstairs, straightening her dress.

Her uncle was waiting in the hall, his hands locked behind his back and a stern expression on his face.

'Balfour is in the library. He has made a formal application for your hand in marriage, and under the circumstances, I have little choice. You do not know each other well, but lots of marriages are grounded on less.

'If I refuse, we have no guarantee that the coachman or someone else who saw you both, will keep their mouths shut, or that someone might one day inadvertently mention what happened. It does not bear thinking about!'

Sarah clamped her jaw tightly and stared at him.

'But I don't want to marry him,' she protested.

Her uncle shrugged and ran his hand across his mouth and chin.

'Balfour explained what really happened, but it's too late, Sarah. I have a responsibility to the memory of your father, and I intend to act accordingly. It is not such a bad match. Balfour is rich and I have heard nothing unpleasant about him. He is in the library and wants a word with you.' He turned away and walked briskly towards the sitting-room.

Sarah froze for a few seconds. It was all so unreal. She straightened and went into the library.

Ross Balfour was sitting in the armchair where she had first seen him that evening. He noticed her dismay, and although his voice was grave, she saw the unmistakeable flash of amusement in his expression as he stood up.

'Don't feel so wretched. Perhaps it is for the best.'

'The best?' The words exploded from her. 'How can you say such a thing? I don't want to marry you. Why couldn't you convince my uncle that it was a perfectly innocent happening?'

He chuckled.

'Well, I tried, and I think he believes me, but it took some persuading. After all, he did find us entangled together on the ground with your dress and underwear torn, and your hair in a blazing mess.'

'Surely he is not stupid enough to think that I'd let someone ravish me without screaming or putting up a fight,' she retorted hotly.

He shrugged and chuckled, his blue eyes twinkling dangerously.

'No, but I think he believed you may have encouraged me, that I was enjoying the situation, and it just got out of hand.'

She stared at him furiously.

'You are despicable!'

His grin was infectious.

'I know! But calm down! Last night I thought seriously about the situation. You told me you want to set up your own apothecary's shop and can't because your uncle controls your inheritance and you are unmarried.

'What if you agree to this marriage, and we request that I can take you away to be married quietly? Your uncle will be forced to release your inheritance, and you will be free to do as you wish.'

Sarah felt short of breath for a moment.

'But I don't want to marry you!'

He reached into his pocket for a cigarillo and lit it.

'I know that, and I'm not interested in being shackled either. You won't actually marry me. I think Marie and my cousin Andrew, her husband, will be willing to help. Your uncle will be glad to get you off his hands when I inform him that we wish to be married from my cousin's home in Pitlochry. You will send them a letter from there to confirm you are in the care of my cousin.

'Your uncle's family are only worried about their social standing and will make up a suitable reason why you left so suddenly. They know I'm about to return to Hong Kong, so I don't think they will bother to find out when we marry, or if I've left with, or without, a wife.

'Your uncle will probably apportion your inheritance to me, and I'll hand it over to you. If you like, and there is enough time, I will help you find suitable premises. You need a suitable male assistant though. Without one, your plan of an independent shop of your own will not succeed.'

Her voice wavered.

'So we don't actually get married? Everyone thinks we will, but we won't?'

He nodded and some blue smoke from a cigarillo circled up above his head.

'Why are you doing this? What happens if my uncle ever finds out?'

'I think it will take some time for him to find out, if ever — especially if you move to another part of the country and don't write letters explaining what you are doing. He knows that in Scotland, once you have been resident for twenty-one days and are over sixteen, you do not need your parents' permission to marry. Your uncle is probably your legal guardian, but you don't need his permission.

'Once he thinks you are off his hands, he won't care what you are doing or where you are. I could see he is more worried about what other people think than what is best for you. One day in the future, when you can prove you are making a success of your life, you can write and inform him. Why I'm doing it? I don't like the idea of anyone being restricted or unhappy. And you are both!'

She stared at him, unable to gather her thoughts for a second, then she made the effort.

'I don't know what to say. Of course it sounds good from my point of view. I don't like deceiving my aunt and uncle. They have been kind in taking me in like they did, but the prospect of being my own master is a dream come true. I told you that otherwise I might be tied to this house for ever more.'

He nodded, and crushed the remains of his cigarillo in the ashtray.

'Perhaps you would have married one day anyway, just to escape.'

She shook her head.

'I would not marry anyone I did not love, and marriage is exchanging one confinement for another. Most modern men control their wives and daughters. My parents allowed me lots of freedom and they had a happy marriage.'

He smiled.

'My parents did, too, and that was inspirational. So what do you think? Shall I write to Andrew and Marie and set things in motion, or not?'

She hesitated for a mere second.

'Yes. Will your cousin be very shocked?'

'Andrew might be startled, but he is a good fellow. Marie? Not at all. She has always been someone who loves escapades and excitement. Andrew is a well-known landlord in the district, and she uses her ample energies to help the local people. She has an enormous sense of fun. Marie will not hesitate to help.'

'What would you have done if I'd refused?'

'I would have found a way of jilting you before I left. I don't like to think how your uncle will react if we don't agree. He will probably imprison you indoors for years, or hide you away.'

He picked up his coat.

'I'll inform you how plans are progressing' His eyes creased at the corners. 'Perhaps your uncle will allow us to walk together, now that we are engaged. Perhaps you can concentrate on the other part of the plan — finding premises and finding a suitable assistant.'

She nodded mutely.

'Thank you!' she said quietly. 'I don't know why you are going to so much trouble for me, but I'm very grateful.'

He viewed her silently for a moment before he spoke.

'I don't know why myself. I think it is because you are one of the most unaffected and honest people I've met.' He lifted his hand. 'I'll be in touch soon.' He put on his hat and, with a swish of his coat, he left the room.

Sarah felt dazed. She calmed her thoughts and gradually a sense of euphoria surfaced as she considered the possibility of achieving her objectives.

She would write to Martin, her father's ex-assistant, straight away and look for a location for a new apothecary's shop. Far from Dundee, not in a big town. Somewhere where people would appreciate the help of a knowledgeable apothecary.

New Beginnings

When the actual day came for her to leave her uncle's house, Sarah felt a little melancholy. Even though the atmosphere was now strained, it had been her home for over a year and she was voluntarily throwing away its protection for an unknown future.

Her aunt embraced her, her eyes glistening with unshed tears.

'I wish you happiness in your new life, Sarah.' She thrust a gold chain with a cross into her niece's hand. 'Please write to me when you are settled. Try to always live an honourable and respectable life and support your future husband in everything he does. Write and tell us that you are safe with Mr Balfour's cousin in Pitlochry.'

After a fleeting kiss on her cheek

from Abigail, Sarah took her uncle's outstretched hand and climbed into the carriage. When she was settled opposite Ross, she looked out of the window and the carriage moved off.

She waved to the three of them standing on the pavement outside the house. Abigail was leaning against her mother. When Sarah looked up, Maisie was peeking through one of the windows and she waved to Sarah, too.

There was silence for a while. She twisted the chain in her hands and felt grateful for her aunt's kindness. She shoved it into her reticule.

Ross broke the silence.

'Marie is expecting us before dinner.'

She nodded.

He decided he had to divert her thoughts.

'You are not regretting it already, I hope?' He stuck one of his long legs out into the dividing space and Sarah admired the shine on his boots and the excellence and smartness of his trousers.

She looked up.

'No, not at all. I've wanted it for it long enough. I don't like deceiving my aunt, but I don't think there was much likelihood of independence unless I left my uncle's house.'

He nodded and studied her pale features that were paler than usual at this moment. She was a pretty girl and showed more intelligence than any other woman he had ever met. She deserved a chance. He did not think she would be single for long. Someone would see her worth — someone she could respect and like.

He shifted uneasily and wondered why the thought bothered him. He was only helping her, and then he would get on with own life again. He might write to find out how she was getting on, because he was partly responsible for the present situation.

'Why don't you take off your bonnet? You don't need it in here.'

She smiled and did so and tried to think of something sensible.

'Did my uncle mentioned my inheritance money?'

'Yes! He just told me he was in the process of sorting it out with the bank. It'll be transferred to my bank account in the next couple of weeks. He is probably waiting to hear from Andrew that you are really staying with them, and that the marriage will go through as planned. Andrew will have to be careful how, he formulates his letter.'

'Your bank account?' she asked, sounding slightly exasperated. 'And how am I to pay for anything if you have my money?'

He laughed softly.

'Don't worry. I don't intend to run off with it.'

She coloured and lifted her hand in a gesture of repentance.

'I'll give you enough cash to travel and lodge until you find your shop,' he added, 'and I'll open an account for you near your new home. I'll pay for everything until your uncle transfers your inheritance. I gather it is enough to cover your needs, and will leave you with a good surplus. If you invest that wisely it will provide you with an annuity that will be useful for any challenging times.

'Your uncle may be an old-fashioned, orthodox man, but he has invested your father's money well and he said it has increased in the period it was in his care.'

She looked out of the window. They were already passing the outskirts of Dundee and the scenery was looking greener and more welcoming. Sounding slightly troubled and knowing she could be honest with him, Sarah turned to look him in the eyes.

'Sometimes I wonder if I'm being stupid. What if it all goes wrong? I still have to remain in the background in the shop, even though I'll be the owner. Martin will be on view, not me.'

'Martin?' He shifted and focused on her words.

'He was my father's assistant and is fully qualified.' Ross nodded and she continued. 'He's working near Chester at present. We've kept in touch, and when I told him of my intentions, he said he would gladly help me and even asked if he could look for a suitable place. If he joins me he will also need accommodation for himself and his family. Martin knows what would be suitable, and if it the location is right, so I'm glad if he starts looking for me.'

'That sounds good. If he did find something he thinks is suitable, you will need to give your approval. He knows exactly what you need?'

'I told him to look for a property large enough for a shop, rooms behind for keeping stock and the blending of mixtures and the like, and enough living accommodation for both of us.'

He nodded.

'I hope he finds something. It will save you a lot of time. You say he is married?'

They were bowling along at a steady pace and even though the carriage jolted now and then, Sarah began to enjoy the feeling that her adventure was beginning at last.

'Yes, Martin has a wife and three children. It bothers me that everyone will think he's the owner, but there is no other way. I've known him long enough to be certain he will be happy with the situation and he will let me work in the background. When are you leaving for Hong Kong? What happens if you've left before I find the right place?'

He laughed softly.

'I promise that I'll set up your account before I leave. I intended to leave in three weeks' time, but my brother has just sent me a request to acquire some spare parts and some new models he read about, before I leave. That means I must go south again to inspect and acquire what he wants, and that will delay my departure by a couple of weeks more.'

The rest of the journey passed quickly. They talked about books they had both read and he told her about a visit to the theatre, to the British Museum, and to an opera performance, during the last time he was in London.

Sarah sighed.

'That must be wonderful.'

Ross viewed her sympathetically.

'Yes, I'm sure you would enjoy such things, too. Perhaps when you are established, you can visit London or some other big city and participate in such events.' He paused.

'I fear that you will need some kind of companion though if you do. An unaccompanied female is still looked on with suspicion these days.' He glanced out of the window. The carriage had turned into a driveway bordered by old trees. 'Ah, we are almost there.'

Sarah surveyed the large grey bricked house with its myriad windows as the carriage came to a halt. The door opened and a young woman passed a servant and came hurrying down the steps. Ross came around to help Sarah out.

Gathering her long skirt, Marie, her

small waist enclosed by a wide leather belt, waited and eyed them.

Ross turned to his cousin's wife.

'Marie! As comely as ever. What devilment have you been up to since I was last here?' He leaned forward and kissed her cheek.

Marie viewed him complacently.

'Nothing much — although I did have a brush with the local magistrate this week when he tried to imprison one of our flock for poaching. The man was guilty, of course, but he has five children and has no work.

'I persuaded Andrew to give him a job hedging, to keep him out of trouble. It doesn't pay much, but he can supplement that with odd jobs for widow McCochran. She needs help in the garden, chopping wood, and general repairs. He promises me he will poach no more!'

Ross laughed and his eyes twinkled.

'You won the magistrate over?'

'I told him it was all a big misunderstanding because the man thought he was on our land and we'd allowed him to hunt rabbits there.' She turned from him and held out her hand to Sarah. 'You must be the young lady this dissolute man is pretending to marry?'

'Yes, and I thank you exceedingly for helping me.' She smiled and received a returning smile.

'Ross explained it all to me in a letter. I thought it was a splendid idea and I'll support any woman who wants to be independent. If my husband hadn't tricked me into marriage, I would still be the independent bane of the local male population.'

A big man, neatly dressed, with long sideboards and whiskers, came bustling down the steps and threw his hand around Marie's waist.

'Don't tell such lies. I didn't trick you — you came running after me, and I gave in.' Marie looked up at her husband and grinned. He turned to Sarah.

'Good afternoon, my dear. I'm

Andrew. I'm not sure that I should support such skulduggery but my wife will have it no other way. Welcome to our home. Please come inside.' He gave her an encouraging smile.

Sarah looked at Ross briefly. He gave her a smug indulgent smile and gestured towards the entrance. They followed the couple into their home, and Sarah relaxed. Her reception was warm. Marie and her husband acted as though it was a normal happening to shelter a young woman who was dishonestly cheating her closest relatives.

Ross did not stay many days, but he did show her some of her favourite spots before he left. They went on a couple of lengthy walks and Sarah enjoyed the expeditions as much as he did. Their conversation did not lag, but they were often content to walk side by side and delight in the scenery.

The evenings were pleasurable hours with Marie and Andrew. They played cards, talked about Ross's relatives, past and present, and the two women discussed Sarah's plans sometimes, when the two men talked of things like politics or hunting prospects for the following year.

In the soft lamplight of the living-room with people she liked, Sarah felt more contented than she'd been for some time. She could believe her plans would succeed at last.

Marie sent Sarah's aunt and uncle a letter stating that Sarah was with her, and would remain their guest until the marriage took place.

Ross smiled when he heard.

'So you haven't given the tiniest hint that it might never take place?'

'From what you told me, their main concern seems to be removing Sarah from their household in case someone heard unsavoury rumours. If they let her run off with you, they are not likely to interfere now any more, are they?

'Sarah included a note that she was well, and that she would be in contact as soon as she was settled.'

No Romantic Complications

A Day before Ross was due to leave, a letter arrived from her aunt wishing her well again. She had included another letter that had arrived for Sarah. Martin wrote that he had used his spare time to look for suitable possibilities and had found two likely ones not far from where he lived at present.

He also told her that when Sarah's father's shop was sold, its new owner had intended to convert it into a drapery. Martin had asked what would happen to all the pharmaceutical equipment. As the new owner had no use for it, and no time to look for a prospective buyer, he let Martin box it up and take it away.

Martin had stored it with a local farmer whom Sarah's father had once helped when he was seriously ill. Martin now offered it back to Sarah for her new apothecary's shop. She was delighted and heartened. She told Ross about what Martin had written and he was silent for a moment.

'Martin? Oh, yes, your father's ex-assistant. Can I see the name of the places he mentions?'

'Of course.' She handed him the letter.

He glanced at it quickly and then looked up at her.

'Gatesborrow? I think that is more or less on my way south. I can meet him, and check on the places he mentions, if you like. It would be silly for you to travel back and forth every time. It is better for you to stay here with Andrew and Marie until there is something definite for you to look at. It sounds like Martin knows what might be suitable. If I give you a second opinion it might save you a lot of trouble.'

Her expression lightened.

'I want to see the places myself, of

course, but I also see what you mean about going on a wild goose chase. You wouldn't mind?'

He shook his head.

'No of course not, otherwise I wouldn't offer.'

'Martin will know what kind of places we need. We need two living-quarters. One for me and one for his family, and the apothecary shop needs storage and working rooms. The living quarters can be over the shop, or consist of two separate buildings close to each other.

'I'll give you a letter for him, explaining you are a good friend. I'm sure you are better at judging the financial aspects than I am. If you agree to what Martin suggests, perhaps you could make tentative enquiries about the price, if you have time. I trust your judgement and I believe you have my well-being in mind.' She lifted her chin and viewed him with confidence.

Ross was taken aback although he did not show it. He realised suddenly how much she relied on his judgement and on his good sense. He was not responsible for her but he had encouraged her to break free. That made him answerable for what was happening.

His feelings towards her were becoming confused and he felt almost relief when he thought that he would be leaving in a couple of weeks. He masked such thoughts and smiled.

'Then that is what we will do. Write your letter and Martin and together we will try to find the perfect spot.'

Sarah felt despondency when she watched him departing in the carriage. Marie was standing on the steps next to her.

'You'll miss him. You two get on so well. I'm surprised, because Ross does not normally tolerate many women for very long. He likes strong women, and I think he sees you are one of those. Most women are empty-headed and only care for trifling things.'

Sarah's cheeks reddened.

'I'll miss him, because he does not

treat me like I'm senseless. We talk of anything and everything together. I could do so with my father, too, and I never thought I would meet anyone else like that again.'

The carriage was almost out of sight.

'Don't get any romantic ideas about him though, Sarah,' Marie added. 'Too many women I know have fallen in love with him, and he didn't take the slightest notice.'

Sarah tossed her head so vigorously her rolled hair almost broke free.

'What a silly idea, Marie. He is my friend, and I admire him for his intelligence and kindness.'

Marie put her arm around Sarah's shoulder.

'Good! And keep it like that. I don't want you with a broken heart. I've never asked him, but I think Ross has left several disconsolate ladies behind on his way through life.'

Sarah put the words aside with sudden good humour.

'I'll not fall in love with Ross Balfour

— I promise! I want to be a good businesswoman with an adequate income, and live where people in the community accept and tolerate me. I'm not looking for romantic complications.' She ran up the steps and went inside.

Ross would never deliberately hurt her, she knew him well enough for that, but even without his doing, love could blossom in Sarah's heart, and then where would it lead?

Perfect Plan

Sarah managed the journey without difficulty although travelling by train was still an adventure. It was dirty and noisy, and the wooden seats were hard, but it was a lot faster than by carriage.

Railways were spreading all over England, and she had to change railway companies a couple of times. Some people looked askance at a young woman travelling on her own and, but apart from a nosy farmer's wife, no-one asked any questions.

Sarah told her that she was meeting a friend, and she did not know anyone else who wanted to travel in the same direction. That was true.

Martin met the coach at Chester and she was delighted to see him again. He had a humorous, kindly mouth, dark hair, was of medium height, and his expression lightened noticeably when he spotted her. They shook hands and he took her valise.

'It's so good to see you again, Miss Courtney. How are you?'

She smiled.

'I'm well, thank you. I hope you and your family are, too?' He nodded. 'I'm so glad that you like the idea of us running our own shop. People will never accept a woman without qualifications. I'd never be allowed to open a shop but I've the means to buy the premises, and you are the qualified pharmacist.'

Amusement flickered in his eyes.

'Yes, you know as much about illnesses and cures as anyone I know. The fact that you're a woman puts all kinds of obstructions in your way. When you served behind the counter of your father's shop, and most people trusted you, some still asked for your father or me, didn't they? It's not fair, but it's the way of the world. It will

126

change one day.'

Sarah nodded.

'Mr Balfour sent me a letter saying that the two of you had inspected some possible sites, and both of you agreed on the same one. I can't wait to see it. He wrote as well that he'd secured a temporary agreement and, if I approve, then the deal will go through without any problems. He also mentioned that the buildings need renovating?'

'Yes, but the position is very good. It is about half-an-hour's journey from the coast. There are several fishing villages along the coast within distance and a lot of surrounding farming countryside. The buildings are in a small hamlet with one main street and a couple of side roads.

'There are similar small villages within walking distance, and the village is surrounded by farms and smallholdings. There's a regular coach service that travels through the village, between the coast and Chester, twice a day.' He smiled cheerily. 'And there is no other apothecary's shop for miles and miles.'

Sarah wanted to clap her hands.

'It sounds perfect.'

'Don't get too excited. The buildings need repair and probably some rebuilding.'

'Is there somewhere for us to live?'

'The largest building would be suitable for the future shop and it also has some outbuildings and a garden out the back.' He hesitated.

'I don't want to be presumptuous, Miss Courtney, but I thought that as there are plenty of rooms upstairs, this would be suitable for my family. There is also a small cottage next door. It has two rooms up and down, and a garden out the back. I think you would be quite happy there. I remember how much you liked the cosy rooms over your father's shop and the cottage is just as cosy.'

'I can't wait to see it all. Can we go there now?'

'I thought it would be better to go tomorrow. I have the keys. You've already had a long journey, and by the time we get there it will almost be dark and you won't be able to see very much. I've reserved a room for you at the inn.'

A little disappointed, she nodded.

'Tell me about this village.'

He nodded.

'Of course. I only saw the place briefly and I must be at my work again the day after tomorrow. My employer doesn't know what I'm doing but he's suspicious.'

Once she had deposited her valise in her room she met Martin again and they shared a meal. Sarah was hungrier than she thought. While they ate, Martin gave her the information he had about the village.

'There's a tavern, a smith's shop, a small haberdashery, a baker, and there are also some other tradesmen living in the village, who have no working premises but work from their homes.

'The people buy meat direct from the farmers when they can afford it, and there is a good supply of things like eggs and vegetables in the small market that's held every week on Saturdays.

'The general appearance of the village is good and the people Mr Balfour and I met seemed friendly enough. We even met the local preacher and he was clearly curious to know what we were doing there, but Mr Balfour didn't give him much information and so I followed his lead.' He paused for a second.

'He is a very noteworthy gentleman, isn't he — Mr Balfour? He gets things done. After inspecting the buildings, and asking the preacher, we took the carriage to sort out the firm handling the sale of the buildings. He persuaded them to accept an interim agreement. He's left their address with me, so if you like the place, you can close the final deal.

'Mr Balfour said he has already cleared the financial side of everything and the people are anxious to sell. They offered a good price, but that's not surprising because the buildings need doing up.'

Sarah was excited.

'It sounds perfect. They'd demand a higher price from a woman. It was good of him to make a provisional arrangement already.'

'Yes, I think so, too. Mr Balfour also left a directive letter with a bank in the nearest seaside town, so that you have an account and money to employ people to get the work done.'

Next day, Sarah saw the two men had chosen well. The main building was long and low, with a slate roof and flintstone walls. The small adjoining cottage was made of the same materials but had received more loving care.

Although the walls were badly blackened by candle-smoke, the rooms were large enough for her needs. The upstairs rooms were planked, and the two downstairs rooms and a small lean-to, that had been added at some later date, all had flagged stonework floors. The walls were thick and the windows set into the niches were small.

There had once been an attractive garden front and back, but both had grown wild. Sarah noted that the small orchard right at the back had several neglected fruit trees.

The main building needed a lot of work, the cottage less. Once the cottage was thoroughly cleaned and the walls white-washed she could move in.

Sarah and Martin agreed she should get this done immediately, then Sarah could be on the spot to oversee work on the other building. They asked a woman walking down the main street if she knew of anyone who would help with cleaning.

She was cleanly dressed and replied politely.

'I'm Mrs Mathilda Clark. I live at number twenty-three.' She nodded in the direction of her home, and Sarah noticed there were some bright red flowers in a pot outside the door. It was a good sign.

'I'll be glad to earn some extra

money. My husband is off work because he had an accident recently at the farm where he works. He needs to rest but he's already worrying. We need to find rent and food for the table, whether he's working or not.'

Sarah searched her reticule and handed her the key of the cottage.

'You can begin when you like. If I'm satisfied, there will be other work. I'll be back in a couple of days.'

The woman's cheeks were like two red apples.

'I'll have it spick and span fast, ma'am, and I'll be willing to do any work you may have for me later.'

'We also need workmen for the other building — a carpenter, a mason, and someone to do general work. I presume the local blacksmith will do any metal work needed. Next time I come, perhaps you can give me names of people who would be willing. Perhaps your husband will feel well enough to do some light work by then, too.'

The woman's eyes lit up.

'That would be a relief, ma'am.' She bobbed a curtsey and set off in the direction she'd been going when they met.

Martin followed her with his eyes.

'I think you've brightened that woman's life.'

'I hope so. Come, Martin, we'll, close the deal on the buildings. We've time before you catch the coach back to your family and your work. I can't say when you will be able to move into the flat above the shop, but I'll make sure the work is done as fast as possible.

'You need at least three bedrooms, four if possible. One of the main upstairs rooms is large and will be a delightful living-room. The windows look out across the fields to the distant hills. There are also one or two poky cupboards that will serve as a storage pantries or wardrobes.

'Talk to your wife about whether she would like the kitchen upstairs or downstairs. I think if you use the end room downstairs as a kitchen it would be very sensible, because that is where the water is, and it will be less work for carrying things like wood for the fire.

'That room overlooks the back garden. You can easily put a large table in there, for your meals. There are also a couple of other rooms between the front room shop and your back kitchen. We can use them for storing remedies, and the biggest one for your work-room.'

He laughed softly.

'That sounds like a perfect plan to me, Sarah. I'll tell my wife and perhaps once you have moved in, and I've a day off, I could bring Caroline to look at it for herself? I know she will be delighted. Our present cottage is very cramped and the three children are sleeping in one bedroom.'

They reached the spot where he'd tied their hired carriage. Sarah felt eager and energised. She nodded to the proprietor of the small inn who was standing in the doorway on the opposite side of the road with his hands crossed on his chest. He glared and turned away. Sarah refused to let anything spoil her day.

Martin soon had them bowling along, at a swift pace, back to the little seaside town where the firm handling the deal was situated, and where Sarah had decided she would stay until her cottage was ready.

Home Sweet Home

Sarah spent the next ten days searching for basic furniture. She bought a Welsh dresser, a wooden table, four farmhouse chairs, and various necessities and appliances for the kitchen.

She found an upholsterer who promised to have two fireside chairs covered in blue brocade finished and delivered by next week. A bed, a mattress, bed linen, lamps and candles, a shelf for the books she planned to buy, a rug for the floor in front of the living-room fireplace, and curtains in cheerful bluebell blue — the list was endless.

She spent the evenings and her spare time sewing the curtains. She decided to search for other gap fillers later, at leisure.

Sarah visited the cottage again and Mrs Clark had kept her word. The cottage was spotless. The upstairs planking shone and she found that someone had whitewashed the walls everywhere. All the rooms were now welcoming and sunny. The cottage smelled of polish, fresh whitewash, and cleanness.

Sarah was delighted. She smiled at Mrs Clark.

'Thank you. Who did the whitewashing?'

'My husband. He is feeling much better. He sat most of the time painting the lower parts and our oldest boy did the rest. It only took a day or two. I tried washing the walls, but the candle smoke was too ingrained.'

Sarah looked around.

'Well, it looks splendid now.' She took her purse from her reticule and handed Mrs Clark her earnings. 'Would you like to help to keep the cottage clean for me on a regular basis? Perhaps once or twice a week?'

Mrs Clark was tongue-tied for a moment and her expression was joyful.

'Nothing would please me more, ma'am. It would mean we could send our oldest boy to the grammar school. He is clever and always has his nose in a book. The vicar has lots of books and has always encouraged our Glyn.'

Sarah nodded.

'I'm sure we will also find some other light work for your husband until he returns to his normal employment. What does he do?'

'He's a farm labourer,' Mrs Clark replied in her sing-song voice. 'When they were moving the bull from one field to the next, there was a disturbance and my Idwal tried to stop it charging off in the wrong direction. The beast grazed Idwal's side and one of his legs with his horn.

'The farmer told him to stay at home until he can do a good day's work again, but he didn't offer to go on paying his wages — the lout! He's a lot better already but the doctor told him to give his leg time to heal properly, otherwise he is in danger of never being able to do any hard work again.'

Sarah nodded.

'Then make sure that he does.' She handed her a few extra shillings. 'That's his earnings for the whitewashing.' She looked out of the kitchen window. 'I think I'm going to like living here.'

Mrs Clark smiled and then spoke cautiously.

'Thank you, ma'am, he will be pleased. People take a time to welcome strangers, but I'm sure that once people know you, they'll accept you.

'Nothing much changes here and we've got used to these buildings being empty and neglected. If there is an apothecary's shop it will be good for us all, and it'll bring more business to the village.'

'What were the buildings used for before they were abandoned?'

'It was a weaving mill. The owner and his wife lived in this cottage. They used the wool from local sheep and made beautiful blankets and shawls, but as they grew older the trade fell off.

'They had old-fashioned machines and faced growing competition from bigger factories. Then the man fell ill with some kind of lung trouble and died. His wife couldn't manage on her own and couldn't afford to pay for help, so she had to close it all down. She sold all she could.

'A fellow weaver bought the weaving frames and anything he could use. I think she went to live with a daughter in Harlech. That was a couple of years ago.'

Sarah nodded and looked around.

'I'll be able to move in straight away. I'll organise a cart to bring my furniture when I go back.' She was surprised that Mrs Clark didn't ask any personal questions. Perhaps she would later, was being polite, or perhaps she just didn't care.

That evening she wrote to Martin to tell him she was moving in and that she hoped to see him and his wife whenever they were free. She also decided to write to Ross. She had the address of his lawyer in London, and he'd told her if she needed to get in touch that was where she should write.

'Dear Mr Balfour,
My plans are taking shape. I viewed the buildings with Martin, and agreed with him that the one you and he found was perfect. The cottage needed no repair — just a thorough clean through which has already been completed.

Its garden is a wilderness and I look forward to the weeks and months ahead when I plan to restore it to neatness and order again.

I've already procured various pieces of furniture and am planning to move in very soon. Martin intends to visit me with his wife as soon as I'm living here, so that she can inspect the rooms where they intend to live.

She will then have the chance to make any suggestions before the work begins.

That is the next step. Once Martin and his family is installed and the downstairs space is clean and inhabitable, we will be able to plan the shelving and all other necessary work that's needed.

We hope we can open for business in a matter of months. I've not yet begun to advertise in nearby villages and towns, but I will as soon as I see we are nearing our goal.

I seem to have spent, and am still spending, a lot of money. We have never discussed how much my inheritance is. I sincerely hope that I'm not exceeding my limit? I would be grateful if you could reassure me on this point. I expect your bank manager will be able to give you a list of my expenditures so far. It is extremely good of you to cover my spending in advance this way.

I have not contacted my aunt and uncle. I think it will be better if I do so when I know that the shop is functioning well and I can prove that I can manage on my own.

I have written to Marie, to thank her for her help. She sent a delightful, amusing reply and I'm convinced that your cousin and his wife are some of the nicest people I've met in a long time.

Marie is another free spirit, but she is also very much in love with her husband — although she acts as if that was quite irrelevant! They are both delightful people.

I hope your business activities are going well, and thank you most sincerely for your help and support in abetting me in my attempts at a self-determining lifestyle.

Your grateful friend,
Sarah Courtney.'

She read it through again and thought about how much he had supported her ever since she left her uncle's house. He had helped her escape, helped her to find the right accommodation, provided enough money to start working, and all without any real intrusion on his part.

She recalled his features quite clearly; his smile, his endearing manner of tilting his head when he joked, the frown across his brow when he was annoyed or exasperated. She didn't understand why he'd made such a deep impression, but he had.

Sarah had never met another man who was so interesting and exceptional. That was not just because he was attractive, it was something more elementary and fundamental.

How often had she silently questioned herself whether he would approve of this decision, or that one, in the last couple of weeks? She was beholden to him, and he'd always sanctioned her decisions.

What did he think about her? Was he

as liberal as he seemed to be, or was he just humouring a woman he met by chance, and that he'd never see again after he left for Hong Kong?

Intruder in the Night

Sarah moved into the cottage. Martin promised to visit her the following weekend with his wife. Sarah insisted that they stayed with her at the cottage. She had already bought a double bed for the main bedroom where she now slept. It meant finding a single bed for the second bedroom, but she reasoned she would need to furnish it one day anyway.

Mrs Clark helped her to make the place look welcoming. There were jugs of spring flowers on the window-sills everywhere, and the furniture had been polished to a mirror-like sheen.

On the morning they were due to arrive, Sarah went to the market further down the meandering roadway. She said, 'Good morning' to anyone she passed. No doubt people were curious.

Some replied, some did not. The innkeeper looked unkindly in her direction. His brow was covered in disapproving lines as he stood talking to some other men in the doorway. Some of his words floated across to her as she passed.

'Huh! . . . single . . . living on her own . . . shouldn't be allowed . . . what's she doing in a place like this?'

Sarah tried to ignore him, kept her eyes ahead, and carried on. She had the urge to hurry, but she kept walking at a steady pace.

It was to be expected that not everyone would welcome her with open arms, and a single woman suddenly moving into a small village like this was undoubtedly a debating point.

She had taken care never to tell Mrs Clark that she, and not Martin, was the owner of the cottage and the adjoining building. She mentioned Martin's name frequently and made vague suggestions that they were distantly related. She longed to reveal the truth but women were denied the rights they deserved. She left Mrs Clark with the belief Martin was in charge.

Sarah liked Martin's wife. She was a pleasant-looking woman in her thirties, forthright and plain-spoken. She had a comfortable figure and small, sharp blue eyes. She clearly thought it was a wonderful chance for Martin.

Sarah had only met her fleetingly once before, when Martin was working still for her father. She could tell that Martin was excited about their future plans.

After they had inspected the building next door, Sarah and Caroline declared that the alterations to the flat above the future shop could begin.

New dividing walls, to make three bedrooms for the children out of longest room facing the main road was agreed on, and Caroline declared the children would think they were in heaven to each have his or her own room. She also announced that the idea of having the kitchen downstairs at the back of the shop was an excellent one.

'What do local people think about an apothecary's shop opening in the middle of the village?' Caroline asked as they ate some of Mrs Clark's Welsh cakes and sipped tea.

Sarah shrugged.

'Mrs Clark tells me that people welcome the idea, as the nearest medical help is five miles from here. He is a young doctor who has just finished his training and is taking over his father's practice. I've not met him personally yet, but I imagine he will greet our arrival.

'At present he, and his patients, have to travel to the coast to the next shop for medicines. We are directly on the road connecting several rural villages hereabout so we will save them a journey. People often walk cross-country to shorten distances. I can't imagine that anyone will be sorry when we open.'

After sharing a meal, Martin and his

wife wanted to return to the next-door building to consider the plan of the rooms, and plot what piece of furniture would stand where, in their future home.

They would need new furniture for the children's rooms, but were now prepared to use their scant savings to do that, as the future looked brighter and more secure. Sarah left them to it. They returned a couple of hours later with measurements written on snippets of paper and looking in high spirits.

★   ★   ★

Next morning, they all decided to attend church together before Martin and Caroline left with the afternoon coach. They had entrusted their children to Caroline's mother, and intended to pick them up on their way home.

The ancient grey stone church was down a side lane. The approach lane was lined with banks of hawthorn hedges, and underneath the branches were emerald-green moss and sprays of tiny white flowers.

The church was surrounded by age-old gravestones, some of the writing illegible, although all of the graveyard was evidently cared for.

They joined other people trooping inside and even if most of them gave them curious glances, everyone nodded and said, 'Good morning.'

The wooden benches were full when the vicar took his place and began his sermon and Sarah was pleased to find it was more about how to live a respectable, upright life, and not a harsh directive or uncompromising command. The singing was melodious and boisterous, the hymns were familiar.

At the end of the service, the vicar stood in the porch to say farewell to everyone as they left. When they reached him he was still smiling.

'Good morning! I was delighted to see some new faces in our congregation this morning. Welcome to the village. I hope you will become regular church-goers.'

Sarah shook hands with him.

'Thank you, and thank you for your service. Yes, we hope to attend church regularly. Mr Wilson is going to open the shop once the building is renovated. He and his wife are moving in, as soon as the living quarters are ready.'

Martin added.

'Yes, there is still some work to be done, but we all hope that will be ready soon and then my family plan to come. When the shop is finally ready, I'll open.'

Just like the ribbons of Sarah's hat, the vicar's white hair was blown wildly around his head by the playful breezes. Sarah decided that his fresh complexion, welcoming attitude, and animated expression gave him a very benevolent air.

'Your family?' he asked.

'I have three children,' Martin explained. 'Is there a school near here?'

'Miss Parry has a small school at the other end of the village. She teaches the small children until they are old enough for higher education. Of course higher education always depends on whether their parents can afford the school fees, although there is talk in Parliament of passing a law that schools must cater for the rich and poor alike.

'At present, if they are clever enough and parents can pay, the children walk back and forth to the grammar school in the next large village. They have to pass an exam to gain a place, or win one of the two scholarships. It is just three miles across the fields, and any children who attend usually walk there and back together.'

Martin nodded and was relieved. His children would have the chance of a good education.

'Good, good!'

The vicar turned to Sarah.

'And you are?'

Sarah hastened to sound friendly. The vicar was clearly fishing for information for the community.

'I'm going to help Mr Wilson with the paperwork, in procuring any ingredients he needs, and assisting him when ladies feel discomfit to have to talk to a man. I'll help him wherever I can. Mr Wilson will sometimes be too busy to do everything himself. He has to prepare the mixtures and potions, and while he does so, someone has to serve in the shop.'

'Ah, I see. Well, I wish you well and God's blessing on your venture. I think everyone is glad to know there will soon be someone at hand who can help in times of illness, without having to make the journey to the coast.'

Martin nodded, but also added a word of caution.

'We can often help, but sometimes a doctor must be consulted. We understand there is a doctor near here?'

'Yes, a pleasant young man. I'll tell him to call, next time I see him.'

People were gathering behind them, so they were glad to move on before the vicar asked any more questions.

'They are all clearly curious about us and your place in all of this,' Martin remarked on the way back to the cottage.

'Yes, but I'll continue to let them believe I'm some kind of distant relation. It doesn't make any difference to us who is actual owner. We will share the work, and I think that the shop will soon pay its way. We'll hopefully live an enjoyable and peaceful life here.'

She went with them to wait for the coach that afternoon. Before they got in, Caroline turned to her and took her hands.

'Thank you, Sarah. Thank you for giving Martin the chance to work independently again. I know how much he looks forward to coming here. His present job is demanding and thank-less.'

Sarah smiled and hugged her quickly.

'I'm just as pleased. I think we will do well with each other. Have a good journey and I look forward to meeting your children. I'll send Martin a note about how things are progressing, and try to hurry things along so that you can move soon.

'You can begin to pack, Caroline! I'll do all I can to hasten work.' She stood waiting until the coach was out of sight.

That evening Sarah was in bed and about to turn out the lamp when she heard sounds below. There was a brief clatter.

With her heart racing, she threw a shawl around her shoulders, grabbed the lamp, and went along the corridor to the narrow staircase.

'Who's there?' she shouted. Her voice quavered. 'Who's there?' she repeated.

As she began to descend the stairs the wooden boards creaked. She heard the sound of the kitchen door squeaking.

The light from the lamp threw long shadows in the low-ceilinged living-room. She crossed the room, knowing the noise was coming from the lean-to kitchen. With her heart in her mouth, she threw open the door.

Holding the lamp above her head she saw the room was empty but the door was swinging in the wind. Nothing seemed to be disturbed, apart from a broom that was lying on the flagstones. She was sure that had been standing in the corner earlier on.

What had caused the commotion? An animal of some kind, searching for food? Mrs Clark had mentioned that there were foxes galore in the vicinity, but would wild foxes enter human quarters? One of the dogs that wandered around the village streets perhaps, or even a cat? Perhaps the door had flown open in the wind.

She advanced warily, closed and bolted the door. She must make sure it was bolted in future.

Her feet felt freezing cold on the stone floor and she hurried back upstairs to her bed again. Sarah told herself it was a perfectly innocent happening, but when she put out the lamp she lay in the darkness longing for sleep, but unable to relax.

Until the early hours she listened to some of the creaking sounds of the rafters and timbers of the old cottage, and realised for the first time that living here on her own might not be just a romantic daydream after all.

Sarah heard nothing unusual during the following nights so she put it down to her imagination. She hired workmen, recommended by Mrs Clark, to make the dividing walls and other work, and she looked forward to the time that Martin and Caroline would move in.

Hopelessly in Love

Sarah felt a warm glow when she looked out of the window one morning and saw Ross handing the reins of his carriage to the innkeeper in the tavern just down the road on the opposite side.

She was taken aback by his unexpected appearance but it was only for a second. Any fleeting surprise was immediately replaced by intense pleasure.

She ran to the door and went towards him, compelled by some kind of involuntarily desire. When they drew close he put his hands on her shoulders and kissed her cheek. They exchanged smiles and he tucked her hand into his elbow as they walked to the door.

'That fellow in the hostelry is a surly

fellow. He has an expression that will sour milk. I almost had to order him to take care of my carriage.'

'I know. He always gives me sullen looks, too. Perhaps he doesn't like strangers, but it's a funny attitude for an innkeeper, isn't it? The locals don't even notice his dour expression. His wife is friendly, so perhaps she's the one who welcomes visitors.'

He looked briefly at the small front garden as they walked the short crazy-paved pathway.

'You have been busy. That was a wilderness last time I was here.'

Her smile was still eager and alive with delight.

'Yes, it was a fight, but I won. Oh, Mr Balfour, I'm so glad to see you!'

Pensively he looked down at her face.

'I think we are Ross and Sarah, don't you agree? We have already shared much together. And I'm glad I came.' He grinned and bent his head as they went through the doorframe. 'I think I can smell coffee?'

'Yes, come into the kitchen. I was just about to have breakfast.'

She knew there was something special about this man from the first moment they met. His nearness now was overwhelming and Sarah realised with dazzling comprehension that, although she had never been in love before, she was helplessly in love with him.

Her mind struggled with what her heart just told her, but she could not ignore it any more.

She turned away and busied herself. What had happened to the level-headed woman who declared she would probably never meet anyone whom she wanted to marry?

He threw his coat over the back of a chair and put his riding-crop on the dresser. He sat down and she hurried to place a plate, and a cup and saucer. She gestured to the fresh bread and scrambled eggs.

'Help yourself! There is plenty more where that came from. My helpful cleaner supplies me with jam and I get other items from local farmers at the weekly market.'

'I can't remember when I last had breakfast without a servant hovering at my elbow. This is very enjoyable.' He gave her a speculative look. 'And you are happy here? Everything is going well?'

'Yes. It is all I hoped for. Did you come especially to see me, or are you on your way to somewhere else?'

He buttered a thick slice of white bread and spread a generous portion of Mrs Clark's blackcurrant jam on it.

'Half and half. I met a young lady in London who lives quite near here. Eliza lives at a place called Plas Newydd. Have you heard of it?'

She shook her head.

'It's a prosperous estate, and her father owns some factories in England. He is a prominent member of the local community and a bit of a philanthropist:

'I met them at a dinner held by a

mutual acquaintance. He had to leave because there was trouble in one of the factories in Stockton, but Eliza wanted to stay a day or two longer in London, so I offered to provide some suitable company on her way home. Their house was built four hundred years ago and is quite beautiful — black and white Middle-Age timberwork, and in a magnificent park.'

'I haven't heard of it. Where is it?'

He paused.

'Roughly twenty miles from here, amidst some delightful hilly country-side.'

'I haven't been here long enough to hear about more than the villagers.'

He nodded.

'Eliza is probably a year or two younger than you. She's an entertaining female, rather flighty and impulsive, but she's not dull. I expect you will meet her eventually. She might even turn out to be your future friend.'

'If they live twenty miles away, I don't think that is very likely. Anyway, they probably move in completely different circles than I'll be doing in future.'

Sarah hated the thought that he had spent any time at all with this rich woman. She tried to sound casual.

'Did you stay with the family, then, on the way here?'

He reached for his coffee.

'He invited me to stay there before I left London, and an aunt was in charge so social conventions would have been observed, but I decided I'd rather see you again, before I set off for Scotland.'

Sarah felt slightly jubilant that she'd triumphed. Ross didn't sound like a man who was enamoured of someone called Eliza. If he was, he'd have relished the chance of staying there. She relaxed again.

'You're going back to Scotland? I thought you were leaving for Hong Kong?'

'I settled some unexpected business with a supplier in Edinburgh. I have to meet him again and so I figured I had time to call on Marie and Andrew again, to say goodbye.

'I'll pass through Dundee, but not leave the train, so there is little chance of me meeting your uncle or anyone you know. Have you heard from him?'

'No. Marie promised to forward any letters if he did write to her.'

'Well, he has been in touch with my lawyer, given him the details of your inheritance and transferred the money. I'll organise its transfer to your account, less what you've already spent, before I leave.

'I've brought the details with me and you can study the papers in peace. Even when you've paid for everything, you'll still have a generous sum to invest in an annuity.

'I suggest you talk to the bank manager about that. He seems to be honest. I think you can trust him. I wondered if your uncle would ask for proof, but he didn't.'

Sarah nodded. Inwardly she couldn't care less about her inheritance — she was too busy with other thoughts when she studied his face. She hoped he wouldn't notice. What she was thinking inside must not be revealed.

A few minutes later, when Ross talked about his visit to London, she was calm enough to add some appropriate remarks. Soon, they eyed each other and were making jokes and teasing each other as before.

She did not know if he had registered the fact that there had never been any hesitancy or caution between them — not from that very first meeting in her uncle's library, or at any time thereafter.

Sarah warned her brain to be careful about what and how she told Ross, and gradually she felt she was not in any danger. He was as candid as ever with her, and apart from talking about personal relationships or marriage, she felt there was nothing she could not discuss with him.

The mist among the trees at the bottom of her untidy garden was dispersing and the sun was gaining strength. Ross looked out of the window.

'I like this place and I like the locality. I can understand what you said about the different temperatures in comparison to the ones in the area you knew in Scotland, but both places have their own attractions.' He got up and stretched.

'I'm going to check the garden out there. It looks like a real challenge.' He removed his coat and looked tall and straight in his narrow trousers, waistcoat and white shirt, as he set off down the barely visible pathway.

She called after him.

'Perhaps you'll get some sensible ideas about what I should plant, and where — when it has been cleared.'

He set off through the maze of neglected plants and shrubbery. Glancing now and then at him pacing the area, she cleared the kitchen table.

He wandered back and forth and looked relaxed as he parted the hanging limbs of the willow tree bordering the brook that bubbled at the end of the garden. Behind him, in the distance, the hills rose in a twisting climb.

Through the open door the air was cool, sweet, and very pure and, apart from the occasional birdsong, it was quiet everywhere.

When he returned, he nodded.

'You need help to clear that wilderness, but it will be very pleasant when the weeds disappear. There's even the remains of a vegetable patch right at the end.'

Sarah nodded. Ross held her glance for a moment before he spoke again.

'I would like to see what the workmen have done next door, now that I'm here.'

'Yes, gladly. I'd like to hear your impartial opinion on what we've achieved so far.' She picked up the keys and they walked side-by-side to the building next-door.

They passed one or two people on their way, or coming from, the weekly market. Most of the faces were strange to Sarah, but one or two already knew who she was, and greeted her.

Inside the former mill, Ross wandered and approved the completed work.

'Martin and his family will live here?' His voice echoed through the empty upstairs rooms.

'Yes, with the kitchen downstairs. I think they will like it when it is finished. I'm looking forward to their arrival. Martin mentioned that on the coach that took them home last time, they met a doctor who lives quite near here, in the next village in fact, and he said he wished he could start his practice here in the village, too.

'He thought that his practice and our shop could go hand in hand, and be advantageous to us both. At present he operates from his father's old practice rooms.'

'A doctor?' He looked at her speculatively.

She nodded enthusiastically.

'Martin said he is a young man with fresh knowledge. The vicar already told us of him when we were in church one Sunday. I haven't met him yet, but he told Martin he would call next time he passes through the village.'

'Is he married?'

'No, I don't think so, but local people seem to like him and I've heard nothing negative about him so far.'

He took his pocket watch out of his waistcoat.

'Are you doing anything special this afternoon? If not, I suggest that we go to the bank and I sign all the formalities for you to take charge of your own inheritance. I would like it settled before I leave for Hong Kong.'

Sarah was a little flustered because she had not reckoned on going anywhere with him, but the idea of spending time with him was too tempting.

'I didn't have anything special planned.'

'Then get your bonnet and we'll be off.'

She looked down at her dress. It was one she liked because the dark blue material did not have a bustle and was not elaborately draped, although the bodice and skirt had attractive edgings in a paler blue. Ross noticed her hesitancy.

'You are suitably dressed,' he pronounced before she could say anything, 'and look very smart, so don't think about changing. It is not necessary.'

She laughed softly.

'How did you know what I was thinking?'

He shrugged.

'Just the way you looked at your skirt, I suppose.' Ross did not understand himself why he could guess what she was thinking. It was almost as if he understood her innermost feelings.

'I am respectable enough for the bank manager?'

'Yes, and if we get through the official part quickly, perhaps we can take a drive along the coast before I bring you back here?'

Sarah's eyes sparkled.

'That would be lovely. When I stayed in the seaside town. I enjoyed exploring it, but I was sorry that I could only walk around the harbour. There was no beach.'

Ross walked to the door and looked back over his shoulder.

'I'll fetch the carriage from the inn and will be outside in five minutes' time. Don't keep me waiting.'

Sarah laughed.

'I won't promise!'

She grabbed a bonnet and a light cape and checked her appearance in the small mirror before she went out and locked the door.

Ross helped her into the carriage, settled into his own place and took the reins. He was a competent driver and they drove along at a respectable rate. They talked about the countryside they passed through, and about Scotland.

'Do you have other relations in Scotland, or is it just Andrew?' she asked, with the ribbons of her bonnet fluttering in the wind.

'I've some distant cousins,' he said, keeping his eye on the winding road. 'My parents are dead. My mother died three years ago, and my father died when I was fifteen. He was a crofter with a little land of his own and he worked hard all his life. He probably had a weak heart because he had some kind of attack one day, and died. My older brother went abroad.

'My mother and I skimped along and, with the help of our local minister, I managed to get a place at the local university. My brother did well and sent money home. When I finished university, he encouraged me to join him.

'At that time he'd already established the business in Singapore. When I joined him he was very pleased, as he is an extremely practical person but hated the bargaining and paperwork. We could support my mother and give her all the comfort she deserved.

'She went to live with a widowed aunt of mine. I think she was quite

174

happy there and either my brother or I visited her every year. Unfortunately she had some kind of serious illness one winter and died quite suddenly.'

'How sad. But I'm sure she was proud that her sons had made a success of their lives.'

'Yes, she was.'

They continued on for a while and were both silent.

The red tape was quickly completed at the lawyer's office and Sarah promised she would return to discuss what to do with the remains of her inheritance as soon as the shop was completed and working.

Outside, Ross turned to her.

'Do you still want to go for a spin along the coast road, or would you rather have tea somewhere before I take you back to the cottage?'

'The coast, please.'

'Would you like to go down to a beach somewhere?'

Her cheeks were already rosy from the wind on her face. They coloured even more when she answered.

'Oh yes, please! I longed to walk on the beach in Broughty Ferry but . . . '

He laughed loudly.

'But then the wind caught your dress and put us in an embarrassing position.'

She joined in his laughter.

'Yes — but today I'm not sorry about that. It changed my whole life.'

The Touch of His Lips

They set off and the road out of the small fishing village climbed gradually for a while until they reached the flatness of the carriageway along the top of the cliffs. From there it sometimes ran parallel, and sometimes wound inland again, before turning back towards the cliffs.

They passed low pitched cottages with slate roofs on their way. All of them were colour-washed or white-washed. The sun was still high and the breezes were gentle and salt-laden.

After a while they both noticed a layover on the side of the road. They decided it meant there was probably a pathway nearby that led down to the seashore. Ross pulled into the verge and fastened the carriage horses securely to some nearby bushes where they began to munch at the abundant greenery beneath their hooves.

Sarah felt light-hearted as she followed him along a well-trodden path down to the sands. She was glad she was not wearing layers and layers of petticoats. When they reached the beach she sighed with satisfaction.

She'd pinned her hair back and folded it into a simple pleat that morning, but now wisps were escaping and framing her face.

She glanced at Ross as he moved with easy grace in front of her. He removed his tight-fitting jacket and slung it over his shoulder.

When the wind rippled his white shirt and outlined his muscles, it quickened her pulse. He was strongly built and his close-fitting silver and grey waistcoat with its gold watch chain emphasised his physique. The wind was also playing havoc with his hair.

On arrival, he looked at her and gave her a knowing smile. She stared up at the sky; it was cloudless. Drinking in the sounds and the colour of the sea, she looked around with pleasure.

Her dress billowed and she bent down and removed her boots. Ross watched in amusement.

'I would dearly love to walk barefoot,' she explained, 'but this is the next best thing.'

He looked around. The cove was enclosed on both sides and they were alone, but he nodded.

'Another time you can come prepared, and not wear stockings. Today, if someone saw you, they'd probably be shocked to find a woman walking barefoot and with a man at her side. They have bathing machines in some seaside places these days, but it is still comparatively seldom. I think it came from the idea that sea bathing is good for the health.'

Sarah nodded.

'Yes, I read about them. It must be astonishing actually to swim in the sea. The women and men are still in separate areas though, to spare each other's modesty.'

'It must be quite difficult to swim when you are hampered by clothing. I was just thinking how my mother might have enjoyed a beach like this. She loved the sea, because she grew up on the coast.'

'Can you swim?'

'Yes, but I do so without the kind of outer clothing people have to wear in those bathing spas. There are some beautiful beaches in Hong Kong, on some nearby islands. Some of the islands are uninhabited so you can wear what you like, or wear nothing. You can imagine that the water temperature is much warmer, so swimming is really enjoyable.'

Sarah did not know if she should be scandalised to listen to him talking about swimming without clothes or not. She could also imagine that if you could swim, doing so without clothes would be liberating. It was typical of his attitude towards her to talk so honestly of such things.

'Do women swim in that way, too?' she asked.

He shrugged.

'Probably, but I'm not sure. I've never heard anyone say so, but why shouldn't women enjoy complete freedom in the water, too, if the place is private enough? There are plenty of inhibiting rules and regulations everywhere, but if you can ignore them, why not?'

He indulged her by walking alongside her to the end of the beach. Her stockings and feet were wet, but she loved every step. They turned when they reached the sheer cliff face at the end of the cliff and returned to their starting point.

They sat down on a nearby rock and she enjoyed the personal contact of his hand and his old-world politeness as he helped her settle down. He was progressive in his attitude and thinking, but traditional in his everyday behaviour. He sat down next to her, and they stared silently out to sea for a while.

Sarah broke the silence.

'Isn't it astonishing? The waves break almost at a regular tempo, and time seems to have no consequence. When someone sits for a while, the sight, the sound and the smell of the sea can calm anyone's misgivings or quieten their worries.'

While resting one foot on the rock and the other on the sand, he encircled the bent knee within his arms.

'Yes, you are right. I wonder why? Perhaps it's because scientific theories suggest mankind evolved from the sea.' He looked out across the waves. 'It's a pity we did not have enough time to enjoy a picnic. He took his pocket-watch out of his waistcoat pocket.

'I'm afraid we must leave soon. I want to drive you home before it gets too dark. I've booked a room at the seaside inn and I intend leaving early tomorrow morning.'

She scrambled to her feet and almost fell, but he caught her. His hands locked around her waist and held her gently. They remained absolutely motionless for a moment, staring into each other's eyes. His stare was bold and approving.

Ross sensed her hesitation, but didn't guess it was because there was a tingling in the pit of her stomach and that his nearness made her senses spin. She swallowed hard, and he disengaged his hands. She remained in an attitude of frozen stillness, but then managed to speak.

'Thank you.'

'You're welcome.'

She pulled herself together.

'Thank you for a splendid excursion. I really enjoyed it.'

'So did I. Don't forget to put your boots on.' He waited, until she was ready. 'Shall I lead the way?' he asked.

Sarah nodded. She was glad of the silence as they made their way back to the carriage.

The journey home was uneventful. They didn't meet many other vehicles on the way. Sarah was calm enough to make the occasional comment about something she noticed, and he seemed quite natural when he replied.

They were outside her cottage sooner than she expected.

'If you are leaving early for Edinburgh I'll not see you again,' she managed to say, trying to hide her rising dismay about his departure.

'I'll call again very briefly tomorrow morning. I'll be passing here on my way to Chester to join a train going north.'

A weight fell from her heart. She would see him again — even if it was just briefly. He helped her down from the carriage and accompanied her to the door.

Sarah fumbled in her reticule for the key, opened the door and turned towards him again. He took her hand and kissed it. It was unexpected and the touch of his lips on her skin electrified her in a way she had never experienced previously.

'Sleep well.'

'You, too.' She watched him return to the carriage, and turn it with skill and proficiency in the narrow roadway. He lifted his hand before he set off, and she lifted her own in reply.

Terrifying Warning

Sarah spent the rest of the day just revelling inwardly in the knowledge that she loved him. She recalled every single moment they'd been together. She would never forget him. He'd had a exciting effect on her from the first day they met.

Her feelings were something she understood better now. She understood that her love for him began on that first evening, and increased every new encounter after that.

Sarah realised that he was an interesting, attractive man, whose intelligence, kindness, and goodwill made him the kind of man she felt comfortable with. He was someone she could respect and love.

After some minutes she knew she

must come down to earth again. She had to concentrate on something that would help to divert her reflections.

Sarah worked in the back garden for as long as she could — until the final rays of sunshine disappeared. She cleared the weeds immediately alongside the path outside the kitchen door.

It didn't completely prevent her thinking about Ross, and she also knew there was no point in sitting in the corner and regretting that she wasn't an heiress, or a woman he found attractive enough to love. She had the comforting knowledge that they were real friends.

Sarah came inside and washed her hands. She wasn't hungry, but made herself tea and tried, unsuccessfully, to read a book. She found herself reading the same sentences over and over again, to the sound of the grandfather clock ticking in the corner of the room.

Resigning herself to a restless night, Sarah got ready for bed. She turned down the glow of her bedside lamp, until there was just a tiny glimmer, and thumped her pillow into shape for the night. She gazed at the shadows on the ceiling and eventually fell into a restless sleep.

Suddenly a noise woke her. She automatically sat up straight, without understanding what was happening.

It took a second or two until her brain caught up with her actions and she noticed the noise was coming from downstairs. Her hands trembled as she turned up the light.

She was too resolute to ignore the goings-on and she reasoned there was there was no point in hugging her bed. She was frightened, but there was no alternative other than to investigate it herself.

Sarah threw a shawl over her nightdress and reached for the lamp. She was hopeful that her appearance would be enough to frighten them away. She didn't want to consider what else might happen.

Sarah crept to the upstairs landing in her bare feet, and was careful when descending. She now knew the spots where the steps squeaked. The lamp threw golden shadows along the walls in the living-room.

Sarah picked up the poker as silently as she could, but when she crossed the living-room and went into the kitchen, she was in time to see more than the silhouette of a darkly dressed man exiting through the door.

She was sure it was a man. The figure was too large, too square, to be a woman. Whoever it was fled, leaving the door open. With a pounding heart, Sarah hastened to close and bolt it. Had she forgotten to bolt it last night?

She turned up the lamp and looked at the latch carefully but there was no sign of breakage or forced entry. When she turned around, she saw the writing on the table *SLUT — YOU ARE NOT WELKOM. GET OUT!* in chalk. She was particularly shocked by the words because she reasoned that the intruder must be from the village, or at least from the immediate locality.

She couldn't bring herself to touch the table and it was impossible to think of going back to bed. Was he still watching the cottage, waiting for the lights to go out, perhaps planning to return?

Pulling herself together Sarah rekindled the fire in the stove, lit some extra candles, and made herself a cup of tea. She felt cold and sat huddled in one of the armchairs for a while, the steaming cup in her hand and a shawl around her shoulders, hoping for comfort.

Knowing that there was no chance of sleeping but feeling a bit more level-headed, Sarah went upstairs and washed and dressed, using the decorative jug and basin on the stand in the corner. The water was cold, but she didn't mind, it helped to steady her nerves.

She busied herself with lighting the fire in the living-room, preparing some vegetables for a meal later, and generally tidying the rooms.

Sunday was normally quiet, because

the work ceased next door. She decided she would go to early morning service. Dawn had broken a few hours ago, and grey mist was still settled among the bushes and plants at the bottom of the garden. Sitting alone in the cottage wouldn't help. Perhaps the solemnity of the church would help.

Sarah went and sat on one of the rear benches. There weren't many worshippers at this time of the day and she hardly listened to the minister's sermon. She still felt too upset. Even the singing was frail and inadequate. She was the first to leave, and she hurried down the lane, along the empty road, back to her cottage.

Sarah was so busy questioning herself why anyone would break in why they would threaten her that she had almost forgotten that Ross intended to call. The relief was tangible when she saw him arriving. She hurried to open the door.

While he tied the reins of his horse to the fence, she had to stop herself rushing out to him. Suddenly some of her anxiety started to fade, but there were tears at the back of her eyes. She told herself not to be a helpless, silly creature, especially in front of Ross.

She must hurry the men to finish the work, then Martin and his family could move in and there would be someone else to turn to if anything similar happened again. She didn't realise it, but her face was full of tension and edginess.

He noticed immediately.

'What's wrong?'

'Hello, Ross! She took some deep breaths of air and felt stronger. 'Nothing. Come inside, I've just come from church and I was about to put the kettle on.'

He looked at her but said nothing, before he brushed past her. She closed the door behind them. His eyes were unblinking. His expression was full of questions. He slapped his gloves across his palm.

'Sarah, stop hoodwinking me. What's

happened? Everything was in order yesterday. Now you look like a ghost.'

Holding her hands together, she cleared her throat. There was no point in lying, he saw something was wrong.

'Someone broke in during the night again.' She nodded towards the kitchen. 'He wrote on the kitchen table. I haven't cleaned it away yet.'

His expression softened, but it was now edged with surprise and puzzlement.

'A break-in? And what do you mean 'again'? Has it happened before? Why didn't you tell me?'

She shrugged.

'I just thought I hadn't bolted the door the first time, and that the wind was the culprit, or some animal. I found nothing amiss apart from a disturbed broomstick. I probably frightened whoever it was away.'

He drew a deep audible breath and his lips were in a straight line.

'And last night?'

'I heard noises again and crept

downstairs as quietly as I could. I saw someone leaving by the back door. I think it was a man. The stature was too big and the wrong shape to be a woman.'

His brows drew together in an angry frown and he sounded exasperated.

'You should have stayed in your room, and not gone looking.'

'Staying in bed wouldn't have made any difference, would it?' she replied hotly. 'I thought he would think twice about remaining if he saw or heard me, and that's what happened.'

Ross muttered to himself and spun on his heel to go into the kitchen. She let him go.

He returned. His face was troubled.

'I think I know who it is,' he declared indignantly. 'You wait here.'

Leaving her breathless, he banged the door on his way out.

Startled, Sarah hurried to one of the deep window alcoves and watched as Ross crossed the road to the inn. His long coat was flapping in the wind. He went inside. What was he doing? She suddenly realised that just because he was there, she already felt protected and less vulnerable. His hands were always waiting to catch her when she stumbled.

She didn't have to wait long. He returned still looking furious.

'It was that crazy innkeeper,' he declared. 'He didn't like the fact that you are unmarried, living here on your own, and getting occasional male visitors — like me. He put two and two together and made five. I was tempted to knock him into next week, but I was calm enough to put him right.

'I reminded him that Martin and his wife and his family will be moving in soon, that you are related and also that you intend to help Martin in the shop, and that you are not some promiscuous loose woman who is planning to set up her business in the village.'

'How . . . how did you know it was him?'

'When I was there the other day, I

noticed he had written cabbage with a K, so I presume he can't spell properly. Either other people in the village don't care, or they are afraid to tell him he's making mistakes. Perhaps he's only had a couple of years of schooling or it's just his weakness.

'His wife joined us just now when she heard the din and, when I explained, she pronounced him to be a stupid dimwit. Your cleaning lady explained all about your presence and your plans to her weeks ago. She ordered him to clean himself up and come across and apologise.

'I told him the least he can do, and as a sign of remorse and goodwill, is to help clear your back garden. He protested about coming here to say sorry, and also about helping, but his wife commanded him to — or else — and he gave in.'

'Oh, good heavens! Why did he get such a weird idea? I expected people would be curious and dig for information, but I never considered that anyone

196

would believe I'm a fallen woman who is setting up a business in the cottage.' Sarah put her hand to her mouth and then started to laugh.

'I expect the innkeeper saw Martin visiting me on his own, and you came yesterday on your own, and he believes you are both customers.'

Ross stared at her face, full of humour, and then joined her as she burst out laughing. His laughter was followed by a generous smile and the atmosphere changed completely.

'After doing my best to save your reputation, I think the least you can do is to offer me a cup of coffee.'

She regarded him with amusement.

'I think so too.'

She made coffee while he washed the words off the table.

'I wish we were able to clear up all misunderstandings in this world so easily,' he declared, with amusement in his voice.

Just before he left, the innkeeper came across and stood at the door with cap in hand, looking a mixture of annoyed and browbeaten.

'I've come to say sorry, ma'am.'

Sarah tried to look austere.

'I'm shocked that you thought so wrongly of me Mr . . . ?'

'Crickleread, Thomas Crickleread.'

She nodded.

'I came here to help Mr Wilson to open an apothecary's shop. He will be moving into the building with his family as soon as rooms above the shop are ready, and he suggested I moved in here to supervise the alterations because I was free, and he could not leave his present position straight away.

'I have no intention of lowering morals in the village, Mr Crickleread. I'm a perfectly respectable woman who intends to help Mr Wilson in the shop when it opens. I think I'm entitled to welcome friends to my cottage without anyone thinking I'm doing something immoral, don't you agree?'

Blustering, he twisted his cap.

'Yes, ma'am. I'm truly sorry if I

caused you any distress and misjudged the situation. I'd like to make amends by helping you with the garden, if you'll allow me? It's a right mess out there.'

'Gladly, Mr Crickleread. I just need help with the weeds and wild growths. I can manage the rest on my own.'

Straightening slightly, clearly glad to have completed the uncomfortable deed, he nodded.

'Tomorrow afternoon, ma'am? I'll get my boy to help and we'll get through it in no time.'

She nodded and held out her hand.

'Yes, that will be fine. Until tomorrow then?'

Mr Crickleread looked surprised by her gesture of goodwill. He took her slender hand in his large paw and shook it. He turned, put on his cap, and wandered down the small pathway on his way across the road again.

Sarah closed the door, and with her eyes sparkling she turned to Ross. She giggled and he laughed softly.

She did not feel so happy when she

stood at the fence to see him leave a short time later. She had a painful knot in her chest, and she clasped her hands together tightly. She hoped he didn't notice the strain in her voice.

'Goodbye, Ross. Thank you for everything. Without your help I might not have found this place. You have solved my financial worries, and helped me to establish my position here in the village and now turned out to be my knight in white armour. You are a real friend.'

Calming his restless horses, he peered down at her intently, like someone who was trying to register a lasting memory.

'It was my pleasure. I hope all your hopes and dreams come true.'

Every time his gaze met hers, her heart turned over, and Sarah was finding it more difficult to stand there, sound natural, and appear as if his leaving meant nothing special. Her feelings for him had nothing to do with sensible reasoning. She loved him and

200

would never see him again. She felt an acute sense of loss already.

'Thank you. Have a good journey. Love to Marie and Andrew, and a safe journey to Hong Kong. I'll never forget you, Ross.'

Sarah wanted to yell, and beg him not to leave. The agony of hiding her feelings of holding back the tears was too much.

Ross opened his mouth as if to say something more, but then shut it and jerked the reins. With a parting nod he rode off at a fast pace down the road.

Sarah watched until he'd turned the bend and then let the tears tumble down her cheeks. She was proud of herself for not showing him just how much she cared. She hurried inside and her thoughts were jagged and painful. She felt no pleasure in knowing now that she was closer to her dream of independence than she had ever been.

After the first wretchedness had calmed a little, she dried her eyes, and sat down to write a letter to Martin telling him about the progress, about her confrontation with Crickleread, and indicating it would not be long until she could report that the work was completed.

Even though it was Sunday, Sarah filled the day's emptiness by cleaning up some of the dirt and dust in the rooms in the future shop. If anyone saw her they would be shocked, but she was careful not to linger near any of the windows.

It helped fill a couple of hours, but when that was completed, and she had finished all tasks she could find to do in the cottage, she made ready for bed, only to find she could not sleep.

Tears rolled down her cheeks. She spent the night staring at the ceiling and wondering where Ross was at that moment.

Plea for Help

Crickleread kept his word and came the next afternoon with his stable boy. There was a lot more work than they expected, and Sarah heard them swearing now and then, but she kept out of the way.

They even had to return the following afternoon to finish it off, but then Sarah could imagine how the garden would look later. She thanked them profusely and the two men were clearly glad to leave.

Mrs Clark could only gape at them when she saw them working in the garden. When Sarah explained what had happened she chortled.

'When I tell other people they'll have a good laugh. Serve him right. Thomas Crickleread has a big mouth and a small brain. He and his wife are always at loggerheads. I was going to suggest that someone would be glad to help clear the garden for a shilling or two, but that won't be necessary any more.' She bustled off with a duster in her hand.

A day or two later the doctor called. He was a pleasant-looking young man, with light brown hair, clear grey eyes and a stocky figure. They shared a hastily made pot of tea and he told her about his training and that he regretted there was no suitable cottage available in the village. He was about to get engaged to his childhood sweetheart and they did not want to live with either of their parents. There was no suitable accommodation in the village where he was at present.

'It would be ideal for me to live in this village with an apothecary's at hand. At present, if I don't have the necessary medication I, or they, have to travel to get it.'

Sarah smiled at him.

'Yes, having the doctor and the apothecary shop in the same place would be ideal. If I hear of anything suitable, I'll get in touch. Perhaps you can ask the vicar. He knows about everything to do with the village.'

He nodded, finished his tea, and put his cup back into the saucer with a clatter. He got up and held out his hand.

'Thank you, Miss Courtney. I'm very glad the shop is coming. I must leave now. Someone fell off a ladder when repairing a roof and injured his foot. His wife sent one of their children to fetch me, and as you were on the way, I thought I'd call very briefly to say hello.'

She accompanied him to the door.

'Thank you for calling, Doctor. I hope you can help your patient and be home again before daylight fades.'

Sarah watched him mount his horse and set off at a gallop down the road. That night she slept well, comforted by the knowledge that any strange sounds were just the ones that all old cottages seem to have.

Next day, she unexpectedly received a letter with unknown handwriting. It was from Andrew.

Dear Sarah,

I'm sorry to trouble you, but I'm very worried about Marie, and I'm begging you to visit us. She's been unwell for a couple of weeks and refuses to see the doctor. I know she respects your knowledge on medical things. She would listen if you tell her there is something amiss and she should see a practitioner.

I'm at a loss at how to convince her. She's so pale, and constantly tired. I'm so worried. I cannot persuade her to eat properly, even when I procure the things she likes best of all. You have experience of various illnesses, and I'm fearful that her stubbornness and refusal to see a qualified physician will result in a more serious ailment. She's so stubborn and sometimes she's her own worst enemy.

If it is possible, please come directly. Don't warn Marie that you are coming, as she will only protest and tell you I'm fussing and there's nothing wrong.

You are the first person I thought could help me. I cannot sleep or concentrate on my work, because I worry about her constantly. If I consult someone locally it would result in gossip and she would hate that — you know what she's like. Although we have only met once, I trust you completely, and I know that Marie does too. I also know that if you advise her she will believe you.

I'm not acquainted with best route for you to travel, but you are independent and resourceful and hope that you will manage it without any problems. I wait apprehensively, and hope you will come to us speedily. Do not hesitate to employ the most expensive way of journeying if it shortens your trip.

Andrew.

Sarah packed, asked Mrs Clark to keep her eye on the workmen, and left the next afternoon. The coach took her to Chester and then on to Manchester via Leeds. The speed of the train made her catch her breath as she gazed at the passing scenery.

In Manchester she spent the night at a respectable hotel that one of her fellow travellers had recommended. Next morning she travelled on, and by early afternoon she reached Dundee.

As the train ferry crossed the Firth of Tay, she looked up at Broughty Castle and recalled the day her uncle discovered Ross lying on top of her with a ripped dress ripped, and her petticoats fluttering in the wind.

Sarah felt like a seasoned traveller. She'd merely reversed the order of the trip she'd made to come from the north to Chester using the same rail companies. No-one bothered her on the journey and she took pains to travel in compartments where there was another woman.

If anyone thought it strange to see a young woman travelling on her own, they didn't say so, or worry her with curious questions. Now she heard the familiar burr of Scottish accents with pleasure although, when they reached Dundee, she pulled the veil on her bonnet over her face.

She only hoped that no-one would recognise her as she arranged for one of the carriages outside the station to take her to Pitlochry. The coachman was reluctant to set out, as the day was well advanced, but she promised him a generous payment, and he agreed.

When they were still on the outskirts of the town, she saw Paul hurrying down one of the alleyways. He didn't glance in her direction and she slid further down into her seat, until she was sure they were out of sight. She wondered briefly if he was still interested in Abigail.

Once they left the town, she breathed more easily. She looked down at her crumpled dress, and wished she had had a chance to freshen herself before she met Andrew, but she also guessed that Andrew was desperate. He wouldn't pay much attention to her appearance.

★ ★ ★

As soon as the carriage reached the house, Sarah got out, and hurried up the steps. A servant opened the door but the sound of her voice must have carried indoors. Andrew came out of the library and rushed across.

'Good heavens, Sarah, you have flown. I didn't expect you until tomorrow at the very earliest.'

She smiled at him.

'Hello, Andrew. Yes, sometimes the speed of the trains took my breath away, too. One fellow traveller mentioned we were travelling at twenty-four miles an hour, and a horse-drawn carriage could only manage eight along the same route.'

He hastened to put his hand under her elbow.

'Come inside, you must be exhausted.'

Sarah nodded towards the driver.

'Andrew, will you please see that this man gets something to eat and drink before he begins the return journey? He was reluctant to bring me so far at this time of day, but I persuaded him it was very important.'

'Yes, of course.' He gave the man a brief glance. 'How much do I owe you?

He doffed his cap.

'The lady has already paid me, sir.'

Andrew viewed Sarah and tutted.

'We must sort all such things out soon.' He turned to the driver. 'Go around to the kitchen door and tell the cook to give you something nourishing to eat and a generous toddy before you set out again. There will be water and hay for your horse, too. Come inside, Sarah!'

She was relieved to have arrived safely. She was tired, but not exhausted. 'How is Marie?' she enquired anxiously.

He wrung his hands.

'No better. She barely managed a walk to the river and back this morning. She was quite exhausted when we returned. She will not admit that she's not well.'

'Andrew, it is at least three miles from here to the river. There and back is six miles! If she is feeling a little under the weather anyway, distances like that are quite likely to make her feel tired. Women are more liable to fatigue than men, anyway, you know that yourself.

'Perhaps she just has a chill and she keeps treating it with home cures, instead of letting nature run its course. I'm sure you must not worry. Marie will hate to know you're worrying and fretting like this.'

'Yes, I know, but I can't help it. Marie has always been so healthy, so full of energy and full of life. She is normally so spirited she even tired me out some days — well, she did until this happened.'

Sarah considered his appearance. He looked pale and his usual neatness was askew. She realised that it was partly because his hair was disordered and his neck-cloth was all awry. She'd try to see Marie straight away, otherwise this house might soon have two patients instead of one.

'Andrew, is Marie resting, or can I see her now?'

'Would you? I haven't even asked about how you and your plans are progressing. Is everything going well.'

She smiled.

'It is. We'll talk about that later perhaps? I'll go up and see Marie and then we will chat again.'

He looked relieved and recalled his duties.

'And I'll tell the kitchen to prepare you a meal and some coffee.' He began to look brighter, almost glad to have something else to occupy his mind.

They were interrupted when Ross came out of the library and strode towards them.

It was so unexpected that Sarah's breath caught in her throat and colour flooded her face as he drew closer. Somehow, she gathered enough sense to speak.

'Ross . . . I thought you would be on your way to Hong Kong by now.'

He spoke to them both, but eyed only Sarah.

'My business in Edinburgh took much longer than I expected, and then I took my leave of the other cousins. Then as I was on my way south again, I came to say adieu to Marie and Andrew and found Andrew so worried I stayed.

'I didn't expect to see you again, either, but Andrew explained he had already appealed to your medical knowledge and asked you to come, so I'm not as surprised to see you, as you are to see me.'

Sarah had had a moment to renew her dormant wits, and if ever she had doubted for a second that she was in love with this man, with pulse-pounding certainty, she now knew there was no doubt at all.

She was amazed by the thrill he gave her by just standing a few steps away. She forced her confused emotions into order.

'Yes, but it is a pleasant surprise.' She wavered, torn by conflicting emotions, needing time to adjust to an unexpected situation. Finally, she was glad to recall the reason why she was here, and that she'd promised to see Marie straight away.

She had a perfectly plausible excuse to escape for a little while. It would give her time to compose herself. She turned to Andrew.

'I'll go to Marie now. I'll see you both later.' She picked up her skirt and almost ran up the stairs and down the corridor.

Outside Marie's bedroom door, she paused a moment to catch her breath and steady her breath. She knocked.

'Marie, It's Sarah.' She didn't wait for an answer but went straight in.

Marie was pale, but her eyes were bright and they sparkled just as gaily as before. She was clearly startled to see Sarah, but she didn't protest.

'Andrew sent for you?'

Sarah nodded. Marie broke into a broad smile. Sarah closed the door.

Downstairs Andrew ordered the meal for Sarah, and then joined Ross in the library. Ross sat alongside the fireplace where there was a big log burning brightly in the open fireplace. He was relaxed, with his legs stuck out in front of him in a straight line and he was staring into the flames. Andrew started to pace up and down.

Ross sighed resignedly.

'Andrew, sit down. Wearing out the carpet will do no good. Now Sarah has arrived, you must wait to hear what she says. I think you are making too much fuss. I'm sure Marie would tell you if she thought something was wrong. You are like two turtle doves, and Marie is too honest and loves you too much to ever to hide anything important from you.'

Andrew nodded.

'I know that what you say is true, but I cannot help it. If you loved someone like I love Marie you would understand better.'

Ross contemplated him pensively.

'You do not have the exclusive rights to loving someone, Andrew. I flatter myself that I do understand.'

'You? And love? Hah! That will be the day. I don't know what temptations come your way in Singapore, but I know that Marie has tried to tantalise you with all the marriageable women she knows whom she thought might interest you. You never once took the bait.'

Ross looked rather startled.

'Did she? I didn't notice, although I should have known she would get up to such skulduggery. I've met some lovely women, here and abroad, but any woman would need to be quite special to put up with my routine and lifestyle. Until now I have never met anyone who I thought was cut out for it.'

'What do you mean, until now?' Andrew was interested enough to have his thoughts diverted for a moment.

Ross didn't answer directly. He got up and went to look out of the leaded window pane.

'Sometimes we expect a great deal from women, don't we? I think I now understand better than I ever have, that women have a right to choose their own destiny.'

'Hmm! In this day and age, in this country, women are still a long way from choosing what, when and why. In fact, I think today's so-called religious morals and strait-laced society mean even more restrictions for women.

'Men can ignore the rules and

regulations if they want to. Women can't, unless they are prepared to live with society's label that they are sinners and reprobates. I think we deliberately imprison women in the belief that the only commendable status is one of wife and mother because that suits us men best of all.'

'You are right. You have not imprisoned Marie, though. She is still the free spirit she always was.'

'I don't want to confine her. I have always loved her tempestuous charm, her compassion for others less fortunate than herself, and I love her for loving me.'

'Then you are fortunate to have found your soulmate, my friend.'

Footsteps interrupted any further conversation. The door opened and Sarah came in. Her cheeks were still reddened, and she walked over to Andrew.

'What is wrong, Sarah? Can you help her?'

Sarah looked up into his worried face.

'I've persuaded Marie it is time she explained what is the cause of her tiredness and lack of energy. I think you should hear it from her rather than from me. Go to her. She is waiting.'

Andrew didn't need any further bidding. He sprinted from the room without a backward glance. Ross straightened slightly as he viewed her from where he stood in the window alcove.

'What's wrong? Perhaps you cannot tell me if it is something serious, but if it is just a harmless affliction I'm sure Andrew and Marie will not mind me knowing.'

'It is nothing serious, although it is quite significant.' She paused and he noticed the humour in her expression. 'Marie is expecting a baby.'

Bitter-sweet Moments

Ross's mouth opened and closed.

'She's . . . ? You mean all this fuss and bother is about . . . '

Sarah nodded.

'Pregnancy causes various setbacks sometimes, like morning sickness and tiredness. Apparently, Marie wanted to be absolutely sure. She noticed that Andrew was getting increasingly nervous and she intended to tell him soon. She didn't reckon with him being so concerned that he would send for me.'

Ross stared at her for a moment before he threw back his head and let out a peal of laughter. Sarah could not help herself joining in.

'And all is well?' he asked when all was calmer. 'She is in good health?'

'Yes, as far as I can tell, apart from

these symptoms, like the tiredness. That particular fact has bothered Andrew a lot, he is not used to a dog-tired Marie. I expect that will even pass in a couple of weeks if she is lucky.

'She says she intends to consult someone who is in qualified in this field of medicine just to reassure him, but until then she is content to rely on the advice of women from the village. She insists they know more about getting and bearing babies that most doctors.'

'Oh, good heavens! Andrew will now probably drive everyone crazy by finding out the name of the best doctor, with the best reputation, and trying to persuade her to see him immediately. He'll explode with delight when he hears.

'I fear that his worry about what was ailing her will now be transferred elsewhere, and he will begin to worry constantly about the various stages of the pregnancy. I wonder how she'll manage to control him. He'll probably drive her mad.'

Sarah smiled and nodded.

'Probably, but I'm also sure Marie knows how to handle him better than anyone else. She will enjoy his pampering, but only for a while, and will then refuse to be treated any differently than usual, and force him to act more rationally.'

Ross laughed.

'You are right.' He eyed her for a few seconds. 'Here we are gossiping and you must be hungry and longing for something to drink. I'll tell the kitchen they can now bring you your late supper.' He disappeared.

Sarah sat in the fireside chair and held out her hands to the flames. She relaxed and was glad of the respite and the silence. She was happy for Marie and Andrew. They would be doting parents.

She tried to avoid thinking about Ross, but it was impossible. Seeing him was bitter-sweet. In was an unexpected joy, but it meant that she would go through the heartbreak all over again, when he left.

It sounded like he really had completed his business at last, so there definitely was nothing keeping him here any more.

Marie didn't need her. After a day or so, there'd be no reason for her to remain. She would adjust to Ross's final departure better at home in her own cottage.

Sarah straightened her shoulders. She must remind herself that managing her own shop was what she had fantasised about ever since her father's death.

However much she would miss the knowledge that Ross was somewhere within reach, and that she'd always dream of him, life would go on. Perhaps she would hear of him via Marie and Andrew. She intended to keep in touch with them.

Voices in the hall brought her back to the present. Ross returned with a serving girl, who decked a small table nearby with a pristine tablecloth and set out the cutlery and china.

She had barely left the room when

the butler appeared with a tureen of thick soup, and some small containers with meat and vegetables.

Ross poured her a glass of wine from a bottle on a side table and pulled out the chair for her to sit. She ate and drank with appetite, while he asked about the progress of the alterations. She had barely finished telling him about everything when the door flew open and Andrew rejoined them. He was beaming like a lighthouse in a storm.

He looked at Ross.

'Have you heard?'

'I told Ross,' Sarah said. 'I hope you do not mind?'

'Mind? Mind? I would like to have it announced from the pulpit in the kirk on Sunday! Marie will forbid such absurdity, of course, but it is such wonderful, and fantastic news. I am so relieved that she is not ill. When she told me we are to have a child, I could have turned somersaults. Come, we must drink to Marie's health and the new member of our family.'

Sarah and Ross eyed each other knowingly. Sarah grinned.

'Well, the baby isn't quite a new member yet, but it's on its way. I suppose you would like a son?'

'Son, daughter, I don't care. As long as both Marie and the baby are healthy I'll thank God.' He handed Ross a glass, and refilled Sarah's. Lifting his own he toasted: 'Marie and the baby!'

She and Ross lifted their glass and echoed his words.

Becoming rational for a minute or two, Andrew noticed the remains of Sarah's meal.

'Good, you have eaten. Despite the fact that it was a wild goose chase for you, my heartfelt thanks, Sarah, that you came. It seems I was too hasty to drag you all this way. You will stay with us for a while and recover properly before you even start to think of returning to your new home. Marie also told me to tell you so. She is delighted to see you again, and so am I.'

Sarah put her hand to her mouth to hide a yawn. Andrew noticed.

'Forgive me. In my own delight I'm not being a good host. I'm sure you are tired after the journey and the excitement this evening. Your room is ready and we will all have more time to talk tomorrow. I told Marie she has to rest, and no-one expects her to come down any more today.'

Sarah looked at Ross. He winked and turned away. She nodded.

'I'll be grateful for a comfortable bed.'

The housekeeper has put you in the same room as last time, and your bags have been taken up. Sleep well, and don't rush down to breakfast. You have all the time in the world.'

Sarah nodded and looked briefly at Ross. There were some things that didn't have all the time in the world. She turned away.

'Then I'll say goodnight to you both.'

Alone with Her Thoughts

At first, Sarah thought that seeing Ross unexpectedly again would keep her awake, but she was more tired from the journey than she realised.

For a while, she stared at the ceiling and knew she was both thrilled and a little upset by seeing him again. She prayed that she could hide her feelings.

It was wonderful to have another chance meeting, but he would be leaving soon for a foreign country, far away and she would probably never see him again.

Who would care for Ross if he became ill? Sarah thought about the jeopardy, the risk, any perils he might face. She concluded it would be better if he found a wife, then there would at least be someone with him who would care.

Eventually she slept little, always fitfully, never peacefully. She was wide awake, and decided to get up, long before dawn. She crept along the corridor to the bathroom. Marie was coming out, looking as pale as a ghost. They were both startled by the sight of each other.

Marie pushed her hair off her face.

'What are you doing up at this hour?' she asked.

'I'm going for a walk, before the rest of the household stirs. Are you all right? You look poorly.'

'Oh, it is just this appalling morning sickness. I hope that it's just temporary. I feel a little dizzy, too, but it goes away when I've rested for a while.'

Sarah smiled.

'I'm not sure about such things, but I think it often disappears after the early months.'

Marie nodded.

'I hope heaven it does, otherwise I'm sure the women in the village have herbal draughts that will help.'

Sarah nodded. She knew how beneficial drinks from natural herbs, plants and roots often were, but that there could be risks.

'Be careful, Marie,' she urged. 'Ask those who've already tried them to be sure. Make sure whatever you drink is not harmful for you, or your baby.'

'Oh, I trust the women. They've coped with pregnancies all their adult lives.' She straightened and looked at Sarah. 'If you want to go walking, you must have my riding costume. We are of a size, and it'll give you more freedom than wandering in layers of petticoats and skirts.'

Sarah did not hesitate.

'Yes, thank you. If you don't need it this morning.'

Marie shook her head.

'I'd like to come with you but I must lie down. Anyway, I've more than one riding-habit.'

'Give me your oldest one, then.' She followed Marie to her room and Marie riffled through her wardrobe.

'Andrew and Ross celebrated last night,' she reported In muffled tones. 'Didn't you hear the racket when they came upstairs?'

Folding the borrowed habit over her arm, Sarah shook her head. It must have been one of the rare moments when she'd slept deeply.

'Oh, dear!'

'I don't think we'll see either of them for a while. Where are you going?'

'I'll take the footpath through the wood down to the river, and if I still feel energetic I'll climb part of the way up Ben Vrackie. The views from up there are spectacular.'

Marie looked out of the long window framed by white lace curtains and nodded.

'The morning mist is still swirling, but it's not raining. Keep to the paths and be careful.'

'I will. I went there once with Ross. I'll not get lost. I hope you feel better soon.'

Marie groaned.

'So do I. My head is spinning.' She half-stumbled to the bed. 'I must lie down before I fall down!'

Sarah waited until Marie was settled and tucked the quilt around her.

'Better days will come soon. Promise!' Marie patted her hand.

'Thank you for coming, Sarah, and later on you must come and tell me about your shop.'

'I will, but rest now.'

Gratefully, Marie closed her eyes, and Sarah crept silently out of the room.

The tawny riding dress did give her more freedom of movement and she set off down the path behind the large house. She looked back at the big grey building. It looked like it was sleeping. There was no movement anywhere. She hadn't even seen any of the servants.

Sarah had pinned her hair back off her face and plaited it, but wore no hat. The freshness of the morning was uplifting, even though grey mist was still playing hide and seek beneath the trees and the shrubbery she passed.

The greyness gradually dispersed and the sleepy longhorn cattle in the fields looked surprised to see a human so early. Everything was quiet and she trod the path through woodland where tall dripping grasses next to the road drenched the hem of her skirt as she strode along.

She almost fell once when a large root, like a thick grey-and-brown snake, burst out of the ground and crossed the path. She only noticed it when it was almost too late.

She came out of the wood and carried on until she reached the edge of the river. Remnants of mist were still busy there, along the embankment. She paused and watched the tumbling white frothy water rushing fiercely over stones and boulders. Sarah pondered if anyone had ever been swept away, or even drowned in it. She also wondered where the river originated and ended.

After a couple of minutes she

decided to carry on and climb the gentle hill for a while. She passed a farmworker carrying a scythe over his shoulder. He doffed his cap and clearly didn't think it strange that another human being was out at this time of the morning.

Sarah took her time walking upwards. There was the vestige of a footpath which she followed. She turned sometimes to look back at the typical moorland scenery spread out below her as she climbed higher and higher. It was beautiful and spectacular.

The landscape where she would live in future was softer and kinder, but as she studied the panoramic view Sarah also appreciated that this was a superb place. Nature at its best. She recalled how she had been derogatory about Scottish scenery when she first met Ross. That was unjust.

She decided not to climb to the summit. It was too far. The walk had helped to quieten her thoughts. She had been here with Ross, and she recalled his enthusiasm. The wind was increasing and pulling at her hair. The weak sunshine was gaining strength too. She stood breathing in the air and enjoying her surroundings. Then she saw him coming . . .

Trip of a Lifetime

Ross climbed towards her, watching her as he did so. Sarah blinked with bafflement and then fought to bring her confused emotions into order. She was glad of the respite before he reached her.

'Good morning, Ross. I thought you were still hugging your bed after celebrating with Andrew last night — well, that's what Marie told me.'

He smiled and his eyes looked greener and more vibrant here, amongst the vegetation of his native scenery. They twinkled when he replied.

'We did celebrate, but I managed to empty most of the glasses of whisky he pressed on me into a convenient potted plant. Do plants get drunk? That one must be very drunk this morning.'

She joined in his laughter.

'Shame on you! You have probably killed it.'

He shrugged.

'Perhaps if the gardener replaces the earth it will recover,' he said sheepishly. 'I promise you that I'll ask him to try. I couldn't escape from Andrew. I spent hours listening to his eulogies and his plans for his future son or daughter. I was thankful when he was so tired that he almost fell asleep where he was. I helped him up to bed. I don't expect to see him for ages, either.'

He stood beside her and looked around.

'This is a magnificent place to be, isn't it?'

It was hard to remain coherent when so close to him. She nodded.

'Yes, I was just thinking the same. It's as impressive as when you brought me here the first time and I take back any derisive remarks I ever made about Scotland or its climate. I have really grown to love it. Will you miss Scotland when you are back in Hong Kong?' She paused. 'That's a silly question, isn't it? Of course you will.'

He studied her carefully.

'It's no longer my home although I was born not far from here. I love returning to Scotland but my life is centred somewhere else now. I hold both worlds dear and who knows what the future will bring?'

Sarah struggled to maintain her composure.

'I understand that. Generally no-one is ever stuck in the same place all their lives, and every location has something special about it. I liked Dundee in the end as well.

'I was reading a travel book about the desert recently,' she continued, 'and although there is often nothing specific to see there, the writer was fascinated by the ever-changing appearance of the sand, and the effect a life-saving oasis has on one when it suddenly materialises like a fata morgana. If you have an open mind, I think you find pleasure and interest in any place you happen to be.'

'Would you like to see the desert?'

She turned towards him.

'Of course I would. I would also love to see Hong Kong, or Singapore, or China, or India,' she added, with dazzling determination.

'Ah, but would you want to stay there, like I do?'

She shrugged.

'You mean not just as a visitor? I don't know, but I think I'm very adaptable and I've always been open to new experience.'

He remained silent for a second and she even heard the wind rustle amongst the undergrowth.

'Would you come with me?' His question came out of the blue.

Sarah gulped and had to clear her throat.

'What do you mean? Visit you there, as your guest?'

His mouth curved into an unconscious smile as he viewed her

confusion. His own expression was all honesty when he spoke quickly.

'No. As my wife.'

Shockwaves hit her stomach, and her lips parted. It was impossible to steady her erratic pulse.

'Are you joking?'

A devilish look came into his eyes.

'No, I'm serious. Just a short time ago I intended to go away and not tell you that I've fallen in love with you,' he said softly. 'You've almost achieved your dream of owning your own shop and I didn't want to destroy that dream. Then meeting you here unexpectedly again, I decided I had to tell you, for my own peace of mind.

'I know that sounds egoistical, and even though you reject the idea outright, I decided I could not live unless you knew how I felt.'

Sarah was finding it hard to breathe properly. She didn't want to deny what she felt any more. He was what she dreamed of. She took the leap and the words tumbled out.

240

'I'm so glad that you have told me. My shop is important — you know that because you have helped me every step of the way — but since we met, I've discovered you are more important than my personal ambitions. I'll gladly leave my cottage and my friends to be with you wherever you go, if you want me.'

He grabbed her, still not believing, and stared long into her face before he kissed her.

Her whole being flooded with desire. Their lips met again and she felt buffeted by the sweetness of his kiss. He looked her over seductively.

'You are sure?' His eyes were full of concern. 'You do not know what that entails. It will be hot, it will be foreign — unlike anything you have known. I'm not always an easy man to live with. Often people and friends say I can be very demanding. Can you imagine being married to someone like that, in a place like no other you have known?'

The idea of being with him for the

rest of her life sent her spirits soaring.

'I could not live with anyone else. I'm demanding and stubborn, too, and I long to see foreign places, so you and I will have a wonderful time.'

He looked increasingly buoyant.

'I've wanted to tell you for a long time,' he confessed, 'but I also knew how much you wanted to be independent, and free. When we were apart, I couldn't stop wondering what you were doing, who would protect you in the future.

'I decided I could not be the one to destroy your dreams. I thought I could live without telling you, but I can't. I love you. I want you by my side. I promise you'll always be the most important person in my life.'

She sighed and smiled.

'And that's all I want. Martin can run the shop. Perhaps he will buy it from me one day. I'll suggest it and give him a bigger share of the profits. The local doctor is looking for a place to live. He can have my cottage.'

Ross threw back his head and laughed.

'Scarcely have I suggested you come with me to the other side of the world, and you are already getting rid of your assets here.' He brushed a gentle kiss across her forehead. His hands moved gently down the length of her back and he bent to kiss her lips again.

Her heart jolted and her pulse pounded. She was on fire. When he held her at arms-length again, questions pulsated through her brain.

'Ross, are we really right for each other? Perhaps I'll only cause problems and difficulties.'

Gathering her into his arms, he held her snugly.

'I know no two people who are more suited,' he said firmly. 'I've never felt so comfortable with any other woman. You make me happy, you make me laugh, you are honest with me, and you are courageous. I'm more scared that I'm expecting too much of you. The heat, the humidity, unfamiliar surroundings, no-one you know, exotic situations . . . '

She laughed.

'Stop, stop . . . they are just what attract me, you know that. They do not weaken my desire to be with you. The notion merely excites me, Ross. You know how I've always longed to see foreign places. With you at my side, life will be brilliant. I love you, Ross.'

His apprehension had lessened and his eyes twinkled.

'I don't know what I've done to deserve you, but I'm sure no-one else will have such a perfect wife and partner.'

Sarah tried to look serious, and failed miserably.

'I hope you don't expect me to sit on the veranda, fanning myself, and waiting for you to come home to me.'

He chuckled.

'No, I don't. European society in Hong Kong won't approve of you working behind the counter of a shop, but there are other ways you can use your knowledge and skill. I am sure you'll make your mark in some other way, and I'll support you.'

She tipped her head to the side, and had never felt so happy.

'For a start, I'd like to learn all about Chinese medicine.'

'Then you need to speak Mandarin. We will find someone to teach you Mandarin when we get to Hong Kong. Can you be ready to leave in just two weeks? There's a ship leaving Manchester that travels through the Suez Canal. The journey will be shorter than it used to be.'

Sarah almost clapped her hands.

'I read about the canal,' she told him enthusiastically. 'It was only opened last year and it's already extremely popular. Bulk transport still goes around the Cape of Good Hope, because it is cheaper.

'Did you know that Stephenson advised our government against building the canal? Perhaps Britain wishes they'd ignored his advice today. He did build the railway between Alexandria and Cairo, though.'

He threw back his head and laughed.

'I should have known that you already know such facts. It will be a honeymoon trip like no-one else has ever known. I'm looking forward to introducing you to my brother and his wife when we visit Singapore. You'll like them and they'll love you.'

'Will you show me the island where you go swimming?' she asked shyly.

'I will, and I'll teach you to swim,' he promised. 'I can't wait.' His expression was roguish, and she coloured. He held out his hand and she placed hers in it. It felt perfect there.

'Come, we must tell Andrew and Marie of our plans — that's if Andrew has emerged. Then we'll disappear for some more time on our own. I can't think of anything I want more. We'll marry as soon as possible.'

Suddenly, his expression changed to one of concern.

'I'm afraid there won't be much time for you to buy bridal clothes, or for us to visit London. I know how much you would enjoy that but I've already delayed my departure too often,' he said regretfully. 'It will have to wait until next time we come home.'

She clasped him to her, reached up to kiss him before she replied.

'I do not care about London, or the shop, or my uncle and aunt, or the rest of the world. I only know that I'm extraordinarily lucky to have found someone like you who loves me.

'I'll include anything suitable from what I have in the cottage in my luggage on the way to Manchester. It's not important to have frivolous bridal clothes, I'd rather have someone I love, someone who does not treat me like I'm ridiculous and senseless.'

He tilted his head to the side.

'And you can always buy what you need as we travel along,' he pointed out. 'Do you know that Chinese women in Hong Kong wear a kind of silk tunic, over silk trousers?'

She smiled.

'Really? No petticoats, no bustles, no confining corsets, no heavy materials? That sounds like heaven.'

He was startled by her words.

'Sarah! You can wear such a thing at home, and I'm sure you would look wonderful, but Hong Kong would be shocked if you wore such clothes publicly. It would be considered inappropriate and dissolute. I was only informing you.'

Tilting her head to the side she stole a slanted look at him.

'I know, but they sound perfect attire for that kind of climate.' Standing on tiptoes she kissed his nose. 'I'll never give you reason to be ashamed of me!' she promised.

He reacted immediately and fastened his hands around her slim waist and swung her around in sheer joy.

After setting her down, he leaned towards her, gave her an infectious smile and kissed her in a way that left her no doubt that theirs was going to be a brilliant, exciting and loving marriage.

We do hope that you have enjoyed reading this large print book.

Did you know that all of our titles are available for purchase?

We publish a wide range of high quality large print books including:
Romances, Mysteries, Classics
General Fiction
Non Fiction and Westerns

Special interest titles available in large print are:
The Little Oxford Dictionary
Music Book, Song Book
Hymn Book, Service Book

Also available from us courtesy of Oxford University Press:
Young Readers' Dictionary
(large print edition)
Young Readers' Thesaurus
(large print edition)

For further information or a free brochure, please contact us at:
Ulverscroft Large Print Books Ltd.,
The Green, Bradgate Road, Anstey,
Leicester, LE7 7FU, England.
Tel: (00 44) **0116 236 4325**
Fax: (00 44) **0116 234 0205**

Other titles in the
Linford Romance Library:

NEVER TO BE TOLD

Kate Finnemore

1967: Upon her death, Lucie Curtis's mother leaves behind a letter that sends her reeling — she was adopted when only a few days old. Soon Lucie is on her way to France to find the mother who gave birth to her during the war. But how can you find a woman who doesn't want to be found? And where does Lucie's adoptive cousin, investigative journalist Yannick, fit in? She is in danger of falling in love with him. However, does he want to help or hinder her in her search?